I0537502

# A Little Bit of Luck

# Luck

Tifani Clark

A Little Bit of Luck by Tifani Clark
© Tifani Clark 2015

Cover Design: Tifani Clark

ISBN-13:978-0692639603
ISBN-10:0692639608

An ABCD Publishing Book

http://www.tifaniclark.blogspot.com

This is a work of fiction. Names, characters, places, and incidents are not reflective of any real life experiences or events.

Dedicated to all those who need
a little bit of luck in their lives.

# Tifani Clark's
# *Holiday Novella Collection*

*One Night at Dornea Pines* (Halloween 2015)
*All is Merri and Bright* (Christmas 2015)
*A Little Bit of Luck* (St. Patrick's Day 2016)
*Losing Independence* (4th of July 2016)

# Other books by
# Tifani Clark

*Shadow of a Life*
*Haven Waiting*
*On Liberty's Watch*

# TABLE OF CONTENTS

# Chapter 1

**B**ree Donovan reached for the door handle, but yanked her hand back just before her fingers grasped the cold metal. *I'm going to lunch with Leslie today. She likes to park on the opposite side of the building. What if we take her car? I'd have to walk out the back door.*

Bree whipped her head around and stared in fear at her car in the far stall of the parking lot. She turned back to the door. Rain still dripped from her nose from the first time she crossed the parking lot. "Better safe than sorry," she muttered as she jogged back to her car. "Always leave the same way you entered," Bree whispered to herself over and over as she drove do the back of the building and parked next to her friend's familiar blue car.

Inside the Shady Elms Nursing and Assisted Living Home, Bree rounded the corner near the nurse's station just as a blond head popped up from behind the desk.

"It's about time you got here," Leslie Collins said.

"Sorry. You know how my luck has been lately. Everything that could go wrong *did* go wrong this morning."

Leslie nodded toward the hallway Bree had just walked down. "Why'd you come in that door?"

"I parked in the back."

"*You* parked in the back? Why?"

Bree opened her mouth to say something, but Leslie cut her off.

"Never mind. I'm sure I don't want to know. I'm just glad you're here. Mr. Hansen is on the rampage and he'll only deal with you." Leslie lowered her voice. "Sometimes I swear the night nurses don't do anything around here."

Bree squinted. "Now what happened?"

Leslie lifted a stack of papers. "Nothing. That's the problem. I'll be doing paperwork all day."

Bree quickly logged into the computer and clocked in. "Don't worry about Mr. Hansen. I'll take care of him. He loves me."

"Everyone loves you, Bree," Leslie said with a laugh.

"If only that were true." Bree grabbed her nursing tools, as she called them, and headed down the hall to Room 137—home of the infamous Mr. Hansen. "Pray for me!" she called over her shoulder before pushing the door open and stepping into the room.

Like all the rooms in the nursing home, Mr. Hansen's room had a distinct odor. Something like sanitizing spray, urine, and a strangely sweet smell she'd never been able to identify all mixed into one. She called it the half-dead smell. "Good morning, Mr.

Hansen. You're looking great today."

Mr. Hansen sat in a chair, staring out the window at the drizzling rain. March rainstorms were typical for Ogden, Utah. With the exception of the years she spent in Salt Lake City going to nursing school, Bree had lived in Ogden her entire life. She knew the town intimately and couldn't imagine living anywhere else.

Hearing Bree's voice, Mr. Hansen whipped his head around. "Finally, someone competent has arrived. If it weren't for you, I'm pretty sure this place would have fallen into a pit a long time ago. A pit filled with alligators and despair."

"I see you're in an excellent mood."

"Hmph."

"What can I do to fix things?"

"Is it too much to ask to have a little something different for breakfast? Every morning of the forty years I worked on the city road crew, I grabbed a doughnut and coffee on my way to work. Sometimes I'd have maple frosting, sometimes I'd have chocolate frosting, and sometimes I had lemon-filled. If I was feeling particularly great, I'd let the girl at the bakery counter surprise me. I love doughnuts, but not once have I been allowed to have one since I've been in this jail."

"You know those aren't good for your health."

"What does it matter at my age? What is it we're trying to preserve?" He pointed to his crippled legs. "I'm not going to suddenly get young again. We might as well not prolong my end."

Bree skirted the remains of the breakfast Mr. Hansen had tossed across the floor and sat down in the chair next to him. "I've met some of your

3

grandkids and even a great-grandkid or two. I think they'd like to have you around as long as possible."

"They're all after my money. Everyone's after my money—not that there's much there to get. Maybe I'll just leave it all to you. That will teach them."

Bree bit her lip to keep from laughing. "How about I sneak you a little extra pudding for lunch? Will that make up for the doughnuts we've been keeping from you?"

"It's a start."

"Great. Now, I need to go check on some of our other friends. I'm going to send Leslie in here to clean up the oatmeal you threw on the floor. Try not to throw anything else at her, please?"

Mr. Hansen didn't say anything else, but he gave a half nod. Bree knew she wouldn't get anything more from him and didn't push her luck.

Out in the hall, Leslie waited with a mop and soapy water. "How'd it go?"

"I told you he loved me. You now have permission to clean up in there." Bree smiled.

"Thanks for your help. They should just assign him to you permanently. It would make him happy and the other residents wouldn't get stressed out when they hear him yelling at me down the hall all the time."

"You just need to make him feel like he's in the right and that you agree with him—whether you do or not. And whether you actually do anything about his complaints or not is up to you. He usually forgets them by the time you talk to him again anyway."

Leslie reached for the mop. "We'll see." She started to walk away, but then turned. "Hey, Bree! You got a new patient today. She got here just before I arrived so I don't know what condition she's in. Check your clipboard."

"Thanks," Bree called without turning around. "She must have taken over Miss Ruth's room. It's the only one open in this wing," she mumbled to herself.

Miss Ruth passed away two weeks before. She'd been there all the years Bree worked in the nursing home—first as a volunteer, then as a nurse's aide, and finally as a nurse. When Bree's patients went home, sadly it wasn't to a three-bedroom brick structure with a white picket fence. Their new homes were permanent and non-negotiable.

Bree sat in a chair behind the nurse's station and picked up the clipboard with her name. Notes from the night nurse filled the page. Complaints, mostly. So-and-so didn't sleep well and kept calling for her. So-and-so needed help to go to the bathroom three different times. So-and-so was just plain annoying. Bree never understood why the girl worked there if she hated it so much. Personally, Bree loved her job and enjoyed going in each morning. She received satisfaction from knowing she brought a smile to the face of someone during what could be their last days on earth.

Attached to the back of the clipboard was information on the new patient. Just as Bree suspected, she'd been placed in Miss Ruth's old room—Room 113.

*Room 113.*

Not a good sign. Anyone who knew anything about Bree Donovan knew she had a tendency to be superstitious. It was already Friday the 13th. Then, to have a new patient on that day in a room ending in the number 13...

Bree took a deep breath, squeezed the lucky rabbit's foot in the pocket of her scrubs, and marched down the hall. "You can do this. It's just a coincidence."

Each of the doors in the facility had a small glass pane in the center so someone—like a nurse—walking by in the outer hallway could see in. Bree glanced through the window in the door of her new patient, but the curtain inside was drawn and she could only see the foot of the bed. She turned the knob and slowly pushed the door open.

"Hello?" she called softly. "My name's Bree. I'm going to be your nurse today." Not hearing a response, Bree pulled the curtain aside and looked at the tiny lady buried in blankets on the bed. Her small body seemed to be lost in the mounds of blankets. A round little nose poked out and Bree smiled as she leaned over the sleeping woman.

*She looks just like Mama Donovan.* It had been two years since her father's mother passed away, but she still missed the spunky Irish woman every day. Most of Bree's personality could be attributed to the grandmother that lived with her family her entire life.

Deep in sleep, the woman didn't even flinch as Bree checked her vitals. She tidied some of the woman's things, slipping bathrobes and slippers into the dresser drawers and repositioning a vase of fake flowers near the window. Outside, the drizzling rain had stopped, and in its place a rainbow crossed the sky.

"I'll catch you a leprechaun and find the gold at the end of the rainbow," Bree whispered. It was what she and Mama Donovan always said to each other whenever it rained.

A sudden change in breathing from the woman in the bed behind her pulled Bree's attention away from the window and back to her charge. The woman's eyes fluttered and then opened. Bree smiled genuinely, wanting the woman's first thoughts of her new nurse to be good ones.

"Good morning, Mrs.—," Bree glanced at the chart, "Mrs. Foster."

"Florence," the elderly woman whispered in a hoarse voice.

Bree glanced at the chart again. Florence Foster. "You'd like to be called Florence?"

The woman blinked.

"I think Florence is a beautiful name and I'd be happy to call you by your first name."

The woman's eyes closed as she drifted off to sleep again. Bree let herself out of the room and headed back to the nurse's station before visiting the rest of her patients. One of them was basically comatose at all times and just needed to be monitored, one had a body of a forty-year-old and the brain of a six-year-old, and two others were coherent like Mr. Hansen, but without his cantankerousness.

She had just sat down behind the desk to fill out morning paperwork when Leslie plopped into the chair next to her. "I need a break," Leslie moaned.

"You just got here."

"I know, but I'm tired already."

"Let me guess, you stayed up late with Jason and now you're going to be useless all day?"

Leslie folded her arms on the desk and rested her

7

head on them. "You know me so well. How long have we been friends now? Forever?"

Bree creased her brows together, pretending to be in deep concentration. "Yes, I believe the correct term is forever."

"I don't get to spend as much time with Jason as I'd like so when we get the chance to be together, we don't want to leave."

"Not much time? The two of you get together every evening."

"Exactly. I want to spend days with him, too."

Bree rolled her eyes, but smiled. "You'll have a ring on your finger by May. And you can mark my words on that."

Leslie lifted her head. "That's a month and a half away. I don't want to wait that long. Of course, I'll have to be engaged forever."

"Why?"

"Don't you remember our pact?"

Bree raised her eyebrows.

"When we were eight, we promised we'd find guys at the same time and get engaged at the same time so we could have our weddings together."

A smile slowly formed on Bree's lips. "I'd forgotten all about that." *We wanted to make a pact in blood, but we were too scared to prick our fingers so we both stuck our hands in the mud and shook.*

"Sadly, at the rate you're going, it will be forever before I can get married if I honor that pact," Leslie continued.

"Gee, thanks."

"You're welcome."

A light flashed on the console in front of Bree. "My

new patient's paging me. I better go see what she needs. And we better find a way to break our pact. I'd hate for you to become an old maid on my account."

Bree squeezed her rabbit's foot and then tapped on the door of Room 113 before stepping in. "Florence? What can I help you with?"

The woman tried to sit up and Bree helped her, tucking pillows behind her fragile back and shoulders. "Water," Florence whispered.

Bree reached to the bedside table and lifted a mug of water to Florence's lips. She sipped through the straw, taking a deep breath after each swallow.

"Thank you," Florence whispered.

Bree smiled and patted the old woman's hand. "It's no problem at all. That's why I'm here. We want to make you as comfortable as possible."

"Red hair," Florence whispered.

Bree put a hand on her curly red locks. Her Irish heritage didn't need to be proven. One look at her and everyone knew where her family hailed from. "It's all natural," Bree said proudly.

She helped Florence lie back in the bed again and returned the water to the bedside table. Before she even had a chance to turn around, Florence was sound asleep—or so she thought. She tucked the blankets tighter around the tiny body and started to step away from the bed, but the old woman suddenly reached out and grabbed her arm with a surprisingly strong grip. Bree gasped and turned back. The old woman's eyes were wide open saucers and she looked scared.

Florence mumbled something, but Bree couldn't hear her. She leaned in, putting her ear right next to the woman's mouth.

Florence's breath tickled Bree's cheek as she spoke. "Beware the Ides of March."

# Chapter 2

**B**ree gasped and jumped back, bumping into the bedside table and knocking the plastic mug of water to the ground. It splashed across the floor, the edge of the blankets, and all over Bree's shoes and pant legs.

"Don't let her scare you," a deep voice behind Bree said.

She whipped her head around, a small shriek escaping her throat. A man with dark hair and a medium build stood just inside the doorway. She didn't recognize him, but he carried himself with confidence and had an air of authority. "Who are you?" she asked.

"I'm her grandson." The man stuck out his hand. "I didn't mean to startle you."

"It wasn't you."

"Grandma then?"

Bree pointed at the bed. "Did you hear what she said?"

"Sure. She said 'Beware the Ides of March.'"

"Exactly. She's warning me about something."

The stranger smiled and a small chuckle escaped. "I don't think that's the answer."

"What's the answer then?"

"It's a simple one. She's crazy."

Bree's mouth dropped open and she quickly looked over at the woman in the bed, hoping Florence still slept. She did. "That's not a very nice thing to say about your own grandma," she whispered. *What a jerk! I can't believe people like this really exist.*

The stranger took a step closer to her. "Good thing for me that she doesn't have the best hearing anymore. Besides, that's why she's in this place. She's losing her mind. That, and the fact that she can't get around on her own anymore."

"I try to treat my patients as if they're still normally functioning adults. After all, no one wants to be treated like a child by someone far younger than them. They deserve respect."

The stranger smiled. "I guess that's why this place came highly recommended by friends of my parents." He bent down to retrieve the spilled mug of water, but Bree jumped in his path.

"I can get that," she said. As she straightened, her foot slipped in the spilled water and she fell backward. Everything seemed to move in slow motion as she rocketed toward the ground. Just before she hit, strong arms grabbed her and lifted her back up.

"You might want to get one of those 'Beware of slippery floors' signs to go with your 'Beware the Ides of March' sign," the man said.

Bree gritted her teeth to keep from glaring at him.

"Thanks for catching me. I'll just get a towel and clean it up."

"An even better idea." He shifted his feet and looked at his watch. "Well, since she's asleep, maybe you can tell her I stopped by when she wakes up. I've got an appointment I need to get to this morning. Nice meeting you."

The stranger turned and disappeared through the doorway as fast as he'd appeared.

*How am I supposed to tell her you stopped by if you didn't even give me your name*? Bree rolled her eyes. Hopefully Florence didn't have a plethora of handsome—*wait...I thought he was handsome?*—grandsons and she'd be able to figure out which one stopped in.

≈⊱⊰≈

Bree and Leslie sat in a corner booth of their favorite café just down the street from Shady Elms. Taking their lunch breaks at the café every Friday had been a tradition since they both started working at the same place, even on Fridays that fell on the thirteenth of the month.

"Is something wrong?" Leslie asked. "You're a lot quieter than usual."

Bree twirled her fork in the salad on her plate. She'd only taken two bites and that had been an effort. "It's ... nothing."

"If you say it's nothing, then I know it's something."

"You'll just mock me if I tell you."

"Ah hah. An answer like that can only mean one

thing—it has something to do with one of your weird superstitions."

Bree set her fork down and took a sip from her water glass. "Maybe."

"Spill it."

Bree knew Leslie would never let her rest until she gave her an answer. They'd been best friends long enough to know how each other ticked. She sighed and launched into her story. "I was checking on Florence—that's the new lady that took Miss Ruth's old room—and something weird happened. I— "

"Weird?" Leslie interrupted.

Bree leaned closer to her friend. "I thought she was asleep, and I was about to leave because everything seemed fine, but then she suddenly grabbed my arm, whispered something, and then immediately fell asleep again. It was almost as if she were talking in her sleep. Or maybe she was in a trance."

"That's not unheard of, especially where we work," Leslie said. "What was so weird about it?"

"It's not the incident that surprised me, it's what she said."

"Go on."

Bree cleared her throat. "Beware the Ides of March."

Leslie laughed so hard she snorted soda up her nose, resulting in a coughing attack she had to get under control before she could respond. "You're making it up."

"Would I lie about something this serious?" Bree's voice squeaked.

"Oh, Bree. It's only serious to you. Everyone else

would laugh about it." Leslie chuckled again.

"Do you even know what those words mean?" Bree hissed.

"Of course I know what they mean. It's from Shakespeare's Julius Caesar. We had to read it in high school, remember?" Leslie shook her head and mumbled, "I really hated that class. Although, I didn't mind sitting next to Spencer Alderun."

"Then you know why I'm so worried. That was the day Julius Caesar was assassinated. *After* he was warned."

Leslie spoke slowly, trying to keep her laughter in check. "You think your new patient is going to assassinate you?"

"No. Of course not. She can barely even get out of bed."

"Then what's the problem?"

"Maybe she knows about something that's going to happen. Maybe there's an aura hovering around me or something. You know that elderly people claim to see ghosts more often than others, especially in a facility like ours where everyone is so close to death."

Leslie reached across the table and grabbed Bree's hands, looking her straight in the eyes. "Don't stress over something like this because it didn't mean anything. Just pretend it never happened."

"Of course I'm going to stress over this. I'm not you. I can't just brush things off. Mama Donovan taught me to take every warning seriously." Bree frowned at the thought of her grandmother.

Leslie let go of Bree's hands and sat back. "You know I miss Mama Donovan just as much as you do, but not everything she said came true. A lot of it is just silly superstitions."

"Yeah? But what if they're not? I can't take the risks. The Ides of March is March 15th. That's only two days away. I could be gone by the end of the weekend."

Leslie clasped her hands in front of her on the table as she leaned against the back of the booth. "Just in case that happens, you better go out with a bang. Want to go out tonight?"

Bree hesitated, eyeing her suspiciously. Leslie wouldn't give up a Friday night with her boyfriend unless she had a really good reason. "Just you and me?"

Leslie looked down. "Uhh ... no. I wouldn't actually be there."

"I'm confused."

"Before you get mad, or say no, just hear me out. Okay?"

Bree tapped her foot on the floor. "You're making me nervous."

Leslie took a deep breath. "I know you hate blind dates, but—"

"Uh uh. No way."

"Come on, Bree. Just listen to me for a second. Jason texted me earlier today and wanted me to beg a favor. An old friend of his has tickets to the grand opening of the new Ogden Cultural Museum. He had a date lined up, but she had to cancel the last minute. Jason offered to help find someone. He thinks you'll be perfect for this guy."

Bree leaned across the table. "Leslie, do you have any idea what day it is?"

"Of course I know. It's Friday. My favorite day of

the week."

"And ... ?"

"It's not your birthday ... so ..."

"What's the date?" Bree asked with raised eyes.

"March 13th."

"Exactly. It's Friday the 13th. There's no way I'm going on a blind date. With my luck, or lack thereof, I'll end up going out with a slasher and I'll be dead long *before* the Ides of March rolls around. If I'm going to die on Sunday I'd like to have at least two more days to live."

"Are you even listening to yourself? You sound ridiculous. Besides, something bad could happen to you in your apartment just as easily as it could on a blind date."

"Not if I'm sitting on my couch in my favorite sweats and slippers."

"You could choke on popcorn, you could have a natural gas leak, a burglar could break into your apartment—"

"Is that supposed to make me feel better about dating a stranger?"

"Sorry."

Bree frowned. "Good things happen to you all the time, but for me it takes a little bit of luck. Lately, I've been running short in that department. I don't want to mess anything up."

"Just give it a shot. *Please.* You know Jason. He doesn't have slasher friends, and he wouldn't purposely do something to hurt you."

Bree couldn't believe what she was about to agree to, but something made her answer in the opposite way she wanted. "Fine. But I'm only doing this for

Jason. If something bad happens, or if I have an awful night, I'm holding both of you responsible. And I'll be thinking of something extra awful the two of you can do to return the favor."

Leslie grinned. "I knew you'd do it. You always come through for me."

Bree waved her hand in a gesture of humbleness, but in her usual klutzy manner, she knocked over the salt container on the table. She grabbed a pinch of the salt and tossed it over her left shoulder before Leslie could even blink. A man in the booth behind them coughed and sputtered. Bree and Leslie stared at their food, pretending not to notice.

"You threw that right in his face," Leslie hissed, still staring at her plate.

"How was I supposed to know he'd turn around right then?" Bree giggled and then lowered her voice. "Throwing salt over your shoulder is supposed to keep the devil away. For all we know, that guy back there *is* the devil."

Leslie raised her head, tilting it to see over Bree's shoulder. "Yep. I definitely see horns hiding in his hair."

Bree glanced at her watch. "We better get back to work."

Leslie sighed. "I know. I promised a couple of the residents I'd play in their chess tournament after their afternoon naps." She tossed a tip on the table and gathered her purse and jacket. "A group of senile grandparents is my only chance at ever winning a game of chess. I wouldn't want to miss out on my one and only opportunity to be a chess champion."

The drive back to the nursing home went too fast.

Bree tried to convince herself that she was being ridiculous, but it was hard. True, she believed in superstitions and myths and legends, but that's only because she had a reason to. Too many times she'd been caught off guard by a bad omen coming true—like the time a black cat ran in front of her right before her shoelace got caught in her bicycle wheel.

"I'll have Jason call or text you so you have more information for tonight. Fair enough?" Leslie asked.

Bree shrugged. "I guess so. Just make sure this isn't one of those blind dates where I'm supposed to show up with a red rose pinned to my dress or something. That's way too cheesy for me."

"If you'd like, I can tell Jason to have him pick you up at my place. That way, he won't know where you live."

"I'd like that. Thanks."

Inside the nursing home, Friday the 13th reigned supreme. From spills, to falls, to lost items, to fights between patients over a game of cards in the common room, everything that could go wrong did. Bree regretted agreeing to Leslie's blind date, but at that point, she couldn't back out. Come what may, she'd be going on a date with a stranger on one of the scariest days of the year.

# Chapter 3

At six o' clock, Bree still stood in her bedroom in the scrubs she'd worn to work. Twelve of her favorite outfits were strewn across her bed as she tried mixing and matching clothes. *Why am I trying so hard for a blind date? These things never work out. It doesn't matter what I wear.*

She tried to remember the last time she went on a date and, sadly, couldn't think of it. She dated in high school and college, but none of the relationships lasted long. Bree had always been the go-to date—the one everyone called when their first choice had other plans or they needed to set someone up—exactly like that night's date.

Bree stared at herself in the mirror. *What is so undesirable about me? I try to be nice to people. I bathe regularly.* She tugged on a lock of her red hair. "It's the Irish in me. It scares people. Maybe I should dye my hair..." she said aloud.

Her cell phone vibrated on top of her dresser, the

sound pulling her from her thoughts. She grabbed it and answered. "Hey, Leslie."

*"Aren't you coming over here?"*

Bree glanced at the alarm clock on her nightstand. "Jason said to be there by seven."

*"No. He said your date would be here at seven. That means you need to get here before seven."*

"I'll be there."

*"Are you even dressed?"*

"Of course I'm dressed. I can't speak for you, but I'm not the type that walks around naked in my own apartment."

*"Let me be more clear. Are you dressed in something other than scrubs?"*

Bree looked down at her work clothes and didn't respond.

Leslie sighed so loudly Bree pulled the phone away from her ear. *"This is a casual date. Wear your green sweater with the white stripes and that new pair of jeans you bought last weekend when we were at the Newgate Mall. Leave your hair down and be at my house in fifteen minutes."*

"Yes, Ma'am."

Leslie hung up the phone without saying anything else.

Bree looked at her clothes-covered bed again. The green sweater and the new pair of jeans were both in the pile of clothes already laid out. She might have come to the same conclusion as Leslie all on her own ... eventually.

She quickly changed into the designated outfit, adding extra deodorant and a spritz of perfume since she waited too long to take a shower. Just before heading out, she grabbed her lucky rabbit's foot and stuffed it down into one of her jeans pockets, giving it a little squeeze as she did so. She didn't go anywhere without it.

Leslie lived barely three blocks from Bree. The pair met in elementary school and quickly became inseparable. They did everything together growing up. They both got their tonsils out the same summer. In November of their second grade year, they both lost their two front teeth, prompting their teacher to make them sing a duet of "All I Want For Christmas Is My Two Front Teeth" for the class Christmas program. It brought the audience to their feet. Together they went out for the track team in junior high and then swiftly decided they hated running.

The pair decided in fifth grade that they would be nurses when they grew up. Most of their classmates changed their minds about chosen professions many times, but neither of them ever did, even when they got to college. They lived together while earning their RN degrees at the University of Utah.

After graduation, they decided that for the first time in their lives, they needed to do something on their own. They moved into separate apartments and got jobs at different places. Bree took a job with the Shady Elms Assisted Living and Nursing Home and Leslie started working at McKay-Dee Hospital.

Their time apart only lasted for six months before Leslie took an open position at the nursing home, but they'd successfully maintained different apartments since college graduation.

Leslie yanked the door open just as Bree reached up to knock. "It's about time you got here."

"I told you I'd come and I did."

Leslie glanced down at her phone. "It's 6:55."

"So? I'm here before seven."

Leslie grabbed Bree's arm and pulled her into the apartment, shutting the door behind them both. "We needed more time to go over protocol."

"Excuse me?"

Leslie took hold of her friend and turned her around in a circle, inspecting her outfit and hair. "Bree, when was the last time you went on a date?"

"Umm—"

"That's what I thought," Leslie cut her off. "You should be able to answer that question without even thinking. You're pretty, you're smart, you have a good job, and no one will ever meet a nicer human than you."

Bree could feel her face turning red. She hated blushing. It made her face clash with her hair. "I feel like you're building up to something."

"But ..." Leslie drew the word out.

Bree nodded. "That's what I thought."

"Your nervousness makes guys nervous."

"My nervousness? I'm not shy."

"I mean your weird superstitions and fears. It's borderline crazy. And you know where I work so you're familiar with what crazy looks like."

Bree plopped down on Leslie's leather sofa and crossed her legs. "If they don't like me for me, I don't want to date them."

"That's fine, but don't overwhelm them on the first date. You need to break them in slowly." Leslie knelt on the floor in front of her. "I've never met this guy that Jason's setting you up with, but his name has

23

come up before. He's a good guy, he's successful, and most importantly, he doesn't still live in his parents' basement. This guy could be a keeper. I'm setting some ground rules for you." Leslie took Bree's face in her hands and forced her to look at her. "No mentioning Friday the 13th, no mentioning the Ides of March—or any other Shakespeare reference for that matter, no throwing salt over your shoulder or at your date, and no mentioning luck."

"Just to be clear, I'm not allowed to talk the entire time. Correct?"

Leslie gave her a shrewd look. "Get to know him with safe subjects first."

"Such as?"

"Tell him about work, but don't bore him with the little details. No one wants to know about changing bedpans. Ask him about his job. Talk about college and compare family sizes. Just don't sound like a ..." Leslie's words trailed off.

"Don't sound like a what?" Bree demanded. She didn't get an answer, though, because Leslie jumped up to answer the knock at the door. Butterflies danced and jumped in her stomach. Knowing the date would be with someone she'd never met made the butterflies feel more like a swarm of angry hornets. *I think I might throw up.*

Bree uncrossed her legs and pushed herself up off the couch, taking advantage of the movement to wipe her sweaty palms on the sides of her jeans.

"Hi, I'm Leslie, Jason's girlfriend. Come in and I'll introduce you to your date."

Bree could only see the back of Leslie's head. The stranger hadn't yet stepped across the threshold.

When he did, her stomach dropped all the way to the floor.

The smiling stranger looked right at her and without hesitating said, "Beware the Ides of March."

From behind him, Bree saw Leslie grab the doorframe. Her eyes were wide enough to cause concern. Bree stepped forward and offered a recently-sweat-free hand. "I don't think we officially met earlier. I'm Bree Donovan."

"Sorry about that. I realized after I left that I forgot to give you my name. I had a lot going on this morning and my date for tonight had just cancelled. I guess I could have saved Jason the trouble and asked you on the spot. I'm Landon Murray."

Leslie stepped out from behind Landon. "You guys know each other?"

"We met briefly this morning where she works," Landon answered.

"I work with her. How did I miss all this?"

"My new patient, Florence, is his grandmother."

Bree could tell the moment realization struck Leslie. "Ahh ... you were the guy in the room when she was told to *Beware,*" Leslie said in a spooky voice.

Landon grinned. "She told you about my crazy grandma, huh?"

Leslie glanced at Bree. "It came up."

Landon reached for Bree's hand, surprising her. "Well, we should probably get going. The museum open house ends at nine and I thought we could grab a bite to eat first."

"I'll call you later," Bree whispered to Leslie as she let Landon pull her out of the apartment.

*Do I want to go on a date with someone I could*

*potentially see on a regular basis? That would be awkward if it didn't work out. But ... what if it does work out? He's even better looking than I remember from this morning—*

"Don't you think?"

Too late, Bree realized Landon had asked her a question. Once again, her crazy thoughts were calling the shots. "Uhh ... what did you say?"

Landon smiled sheepishly. "I mentioned the weather. Sorry. It was tacky. I'm really bad at this whole blind date thing."

Bree focused on him. "Me, too. You're the first guy I've agreed to go on a blind date with in ... years."

"I feel pretty special then."

Bree tossed her hair over her shoulder. "You should." *I'm doing it! I'm flirting! Leslie would be so proud.*

Landon opened the passenger door of what looked to be a brand new car. Bree slid across the black leather seat, admiring the interior as he walked around to his side of the car.

"So, you know what I do for a living, what do you do?" she asked.

"I'm a consultant."

"For ... ?"

"Many different people."

"That's a pretty vague answer. Are you secretly telling me you're a drug dealer?"

Landon laughed and put his arm on the back of her chair while he reversed. She caught a whiff of his cologne and she liked it. A lot. "I'm not trying to be vague, I just don't want to bore you. Jason told me you were a girl I didn't want to miss out on and I wasn't

26

allowed to be boring."

"Hmm … I got the same lecture from Leslie."

"Sounds like we're both a little rusty."

Bree buckled her seatbelt. "That's an understatement."

"How about we ignore everything they told us and just be ourselves?"

"I'd like that. I've already forgotten all the things Leslie told me were safe topics anyway."

Landon kept one hand on the wheel while the other casually rested on his leg. From the side angle, Bree could see a dimple in his right cheek, giving him a boyish look. "To answer your earlier question," he began, "I'm a business efficiency consultant. I work for a company based here in Ogden, but we travel all over for different clients."

"What exactly does a business-something-something do?"

Landon turned and grinned at her. "A business efficiency consultant. We go to businesses who are trying to trim the fat and study their company. We tell them ways they could do things more efficiently to save money. Basically, they pay me money in order to save money."

"Are you the guy that decides who gets fired?"

Landon hesitated. "Sometimes. I don't ever do the actual firing. That's left up to the company heads, but … sometimes my recommendations are to let certain people go. It doesn't usually come down to that. If I'm successful, I can find ways for them to cut spending without anyone losing a job."

"It sounds interesting."

"You don't have to be nice. It's not all that exciting.

I'm surprised you didn't fall asleep while listening to me just now." He glanced at her before returning his eyes to the road. "I'm sure my days aren't nearly as interesting as yours."

"I do the exact same thing every day."

"You don't like being a nurse?"

"Oh no, I love it. It's just not exciting and glamorous."

"Trust me, my job isn't glamorous," Landon said. "And I'd be willing to bet you have some pretty crazy stories to tell."

A smile came to Bree's lips. "That's true. There are definitely moments."

"Like my grandmother today?"

"Exactly."

"You seemed pretty shaken by the Ides of March thing. Are you superstitious?"

*Uh oh. We haven't even gotten to the restaurant and the taboo topic is already on the table.* She hesitated before answering. "Maybe a little." *Now that's an understatement.*

"Nothing wrong with that, I guess. It probably keeps your life interesting."

*Ha! Take that, Leslie! Being superstitious keeps life interesting!* "What about you?"

He shook his head. "I don't believe in any of that stuff. Luck isn't real. Things happen to people because of choices they make. Luck has nothing to do with it."

*He doesn't believe in luck? This might be a deal breaker.*

# Chapter 4

**B**ree remained quiet, contemplating the fact that Landon didn't believe in luck, as he circled the parking lot of a local steakhouse. It looked as if everyone in Ogden opted to eat there that night.

"Don't worry. I made reservations so I don't think we'll have much of a wait once we find a parking spot," Landon said. He finally found an empty stall in the back and pulled in, shifting into park smoothly.

Bree continued to keep her silence as she waited for him to come around to her side to open her door. He'd shown earlier that he was a gentleman and she appreciated that fact.

"Have you ever been here?" he asked casually as they approached the front door.

Bree kept her eyes on the ground, carefully watching each step she took. "Once or twice. How about you?"

"I've never eaten here, but Jason recommended it. He has good taste so I figured I'd give it a try."

"I think you'll like it."

Inside, Landon gave his name to the hostess and they were promptly seated at a quiet table for two in the back of the building. "Wow. You got lucky. These tables are hard to get from what I hear."

Landon leaned forward. "Luck has nothing to do with it. I just know how to get what I want."

Bree narrowed her eyes at him. "So you're saying you're pushy?"

Landon threw his head back and laughed. "No. Actually, when I called in, they said they'd just had a cancellation."

"Ah hah!" Bree cried, a little too loud. She lowered her voice. "That was luck. *You* got lucky."

"It wasn't luck, it was perfect timing."

"That's luck."

Landon put up his hands. "I beg to differ."

Each of them ordered a steak dinner with two sides. Landon's dateability level rose a little when he ordered two different vegetables as his sides. Bree could never be with a guy who didn't eat something healthy once in a while. Of course, not believing in luck still kept him scraping bottom.

They chatted and chewed and laughed and talked. Bree hated to admit it to herself, but she felt comfortable around Landon. Considering how long she'd known him, it was something that shocked her. During one particularly entertaining retelling—on her part—of an incident at the nursing home, she accidentally knocked her steak knife to the ground. Embarrassed, she stared at the knife, wondering how she could kick it under her table without anyone noticing ... and how she could ask for a new knife without being too obvious.

"Here," Landon said. "This one's clean."

Bree looked up and saw him holding out a knife. "You saw that, huh?"

"It happens to the best of us. I had two for some reason. This is an extra." He stuck his hand out again, offering the knife.

"Thanks. Just set it on the table."

He shrugged and set the knife on the table. "Afraid you might accidentally touch me?" he teased.

Bree picked up her water glass and took a big gulp, hoping the ice water would cool her cheeks before they had time to turn red. It didn't work. "No. It's just ... nothing."

"Nothing? Now I'm curious. You have to tell me."

"You sound like Leslie."

"Tonight was the first time I met her so I don't know if that's a good thing or a bad thing."

"It's a little of both."

"Ouch." He cringed. "So tell me, why can't I hand you the knife?"

"It's ... umm ... bad luck. You should never hand someone a knife. You set it on the table and let them pick it up."

"I'm not sure if luck has anything to do with it, but I guess it makes sense for safety reasons."

"It's just something Mama Donovan used to say all the time."

Landon raised his eyebrows. "Mama who?"

"Mama Donovan. She is ... was ... my father's mother."

"Sounds like an interesting woman."

"Oh she was. Believe me."

31

"Did she have the same view of luck as you?" Landon asked.

Bree smiled. "I've been told many times that I'm exactly like her. I take that as a compliment. She passed away a couple of years ago."

"It sounds like the two of you were close."

Bree fingered the edge of the tablecloth. "We were. She lived with my parents and me my entire life. She grew up in Ireland and then immigrated here when she was nineteen. My dad's never been that interested in his heritage and she didn't want it to die with her. She focused a lot of her energy on teaching me the traditions of our ancestors."

Landon pushed his plate away and leaned forward. "So your grandma *is* the one to blame for your belief in luck and superstitions. I should have known you were Irish."

"The red hair didn't give it away? You say it like it's a bad thing."

Landon quickly shook his head. "No. Not at all. I actually find it interesting to see how everyone's heritage shapes their personalities. And, on top of that, I'm kind of partial to red hair."

Bree looked down at her plate, trying to hide another smile. *He's not so bad. Maybe I can convince him that there's truth to my ideas.*

Landon cleared his throat. "We should probably get going if we're going to make it to the museum event. It's an open house, but we should probably leave ourselves enough time to see the exhibits."

"How did you score an invitation to opening night?" Bree asked as she stood. Landon helped her with her jacket and she smiled to herself at his nearness.

"They hired me to do an efficiency consultation before they opened to make sure everything started off as smoothly as possible. They sent invitations to anyone who helped behind the scenes."

"Makes sense. Your job has perks."

He put a hand on the small of her back and led her toward the restaurant doors. "You could say that."

"The only invitations I get from my clients are funeral announcements."

Inside Landon's car, Bree snuggled back against the buttery leather seat. Landon seemed like a great guy. He had a good job and wouldn't rely on her for everything ... just as Leslie promised. And his looks were nothing to complain about, either. *If I can just convince him that luck is real and that I've somehow lost the luck of the Irish, this guy wouldn't be half bad.*

Halfway to the new museum, Bree's phone buzzed in her pocket. She tried to pull it out casually, knowing it would be rude to focus on her phone on a date, but as she slipped it out of her back pocket, it fell down between the door and the seat with a big clunk. *Of all the luck ...* Bree stared out the window, wondering how to retrieve it without drawing attention.

"Are you going to get that?" Landon asked.

"Get what?"

"Your phone. You dropped it."

"Did I?"

Landon laughed. "You can check it. I won't be offended."

"Sorry." Bree reached down and felt around for her phone. Just before she looked up, a loud thunk from the front of the car startled her and she jumped back against the seat. Landon cursed under his breath.

"What was *that*?" she asked in a panic.

"A stupid bird flew out in front of us. I hope it didn't dent my car. I've only had this for a month."

Bree felt the color drain from her face. "A ... bird?"

Landon nodded.

"What kind?"

"Don't know. It's too dark to tell what it was."

Bree swallowed hard. "We have to go back."

"Back? Where?"

"We have to check on the bird," Bree demanded.

"Oh."

Silence.

"What does 'oh' mean?" Bree asked, a little more forcefully than she intended.

"I didn't know you were an animal activist. I promise I have nothing against animals. It flew out of nowhere. Anyone would have hit it."

"It's not that. I mean, I like animals just fine, but ... I just need to know what kind of bird it was ... and if it died."

Landon watched her for a long moment before shaking his head and flipping a U-turn.

*That's the end of this relationship. Over before the date even ended. He'll know I'm crazy for sure now. I hope he doesn't tell Jason why he doesn't want to keep dating me. Jason will tell Leslie and then Leslie will lecture me—again.*

Landon slowed the car down and pulled to the side of the road. "I think we were somewhere around here."

Bree jumped from the car and began scouring the sidewalk for a dead bird, hoping she wouldn't find one since that would lead her to conclude that the bird lived and flew away on its merry way. Back by the car, Landon examined the front of his car, carefully searching for dents.

"How's your car?" Bree called.

"It's fine. Just a few feathers."

Bree cringed. "That can't be good."

"Hey, I think the bird is over here in the gutter," he called back.

Bree straightened and looked where he pointed. She couldn't make out anything but a dark shadow. Her heart raced and she closed her eyes. "Can you tell what kind it is?" She peeked through the slits between her eyelids as Landon aimed his cell phone light at the ground.

"I'm not an expert, but I'm pretty sure it's a robin."

"No!" Bree groaned.

"Don't worry. They're not on the endangered list."

"If you kill a robin, you kill your luck for the rest of your life."

Landon started to laugh, but then quickly stopped when he noted the expression on Bree's face. He stepped toward her and put his hands on her shoulders. "Bree, there's no such thing as luck. You're fine. Besides, I was the one driving the car, so wouldn't it be me who has a lifetime of cursed luck?"

Bree stared at the ground. "Mama Donovan always said robins are bad omens. They can even mean impending death. This is the second death omen I've had today. I'm not going to make it to see my next birthday."

Landon stepped back from her and folded his arms over his chest. "That's it. I'm making you my new project."

"Excuse me?"

"You're fun to talk to, pretty as Jason promised, and you've got an Irish streak that totally intrigues me. I'm going to cure you of your fears and superstitions."

"You're making me your *project*?" Bree hissed.

"That's what I do, remember?" Landon said. "I make recommendations and help people fix problems."

"I can't believe I'm hearing this. I'm not a problem, but you apparently are."

"You're taking this the wrong way." Landon reached for her, but Bree stepped back.

"I'll just call Leslie to come get me. You don't need to take me home." She turned around and began walking away from him down the sidewalk."

"Aren't you forgetting something?"

"Go to the museum alone!" she called without turning around.

"What about your purse? And did you get the phone you dropped down the side of my car?"

Bree stopped walking and took a deep breath before turning around. When she did turn, Landon had closed the distance between them without making a noise and stood only a foot away. Her heart fluttered in her chest.

"I've totally botched this, but I think you should hear me out anyway," he insisted. "If you're still mad and don't agree with me, I'll take you right back to Leslie's place."

Bree crossed her arms over her chest, mimicking his stance. "Go ahead."

"I know I just barely met you, but part of my job is to be observant. I notice the little details. This morning, when I first met you, I know that my grandma's crazy mutterings terrified you. I could see it in your eyes. At the time, I thought the terror came from surprise at her sudden movement, but it wasn't. You've admitted to believing in luck, which I don't agree with, but whatever. At the restaurant, you wouldn't let me hand you a knife. Walking into the restaurant and out of the restaurant you kept your head down to make sure you didn't step on a single crack in the sidewalk. Sure, we all played that game in elementary school, but you obviously haven't let it go. And now there's a dead robin and you're freaking out. Your obsession with superstitions and luck is borderline psycho."

Bree's mouth dropped open and she considered punching him. "How dare—"

"You didn't let me finish," Landon said, cutting her off. "I find all of it kind of cute. You're a girl that knows what you like and what you want and you don't say things just to please a guy. I like that."

"Now that you've completely put me down, will you take me back to Leslie's?"

"No. I'm not through. Usually I spend at least a week with a company before making any recommendations. All I ask is that you give me one weekend. Saturday and Sunday. Two days. Spend all your time with me and I'll convince you that there's no truth to these superstitions."

"And what if I convince you that there is?"

"Then I guess you win."

"What do you get from this? I'm not paying you to

make fun of me for two days."

Landon grinned. "I get the satisfaction of knowing that I proved something to you … and I get to hang out with a hot girl for two days."

A smile tried to escape, but Bree quickly shoved it back down. "It would never work. I work one Sunday a month and this is my Sunday on. Besides, according to your grandmother, I'm going to die that day."

"I'll just hang out with Grandma while you're on duty. And if you die, I'll be there to mourn your passing."

"Wouldn't this be considered a form of stalking?"

"Not if we both know about each other's presence and we agree to it."

As frustrating as Landon had proved to be, something in the back of Bree's head urged her to agree to his crazy idea. She knew part of it had to do with his charm, but part of it had to do with her desire to prove him wrong and wipe the smile from his face. "Fine. You have two days."

# Chapter 5

After the too-long encounter on the side of an Ogden side street, Bree and Landon went home without going to the museum opening. Bree felt bad making him miss it, but by the time they finished arguing on the sidewalk, there were only ten short minutes left at the gala. *Serves him right*, she thought as she woke up the next morning.

She stretched each muscle slowly before climbing out of bed, a ritual she completed every morning. She'd done it for so long, she couldn't remember if there was any superstitious reason behind it or if it just felt good to wake up that way.

She swung her legs over the side of her bed—the same side she always got up from—and reached for her blinking phone on the side of her bed. She'd turned the phone to vibrate after she got home, not wanting to be bothered. Looking at the screen, she saw notifications for three missed calls and four texts—all from Leslie.

She read the last text out loud. "I'm guessing since you aren't returning my calls and it's now midnight and you haven't come back here, you let him know your real address. That means the date went well. Can't wait to hear about it. Talk to you tomorrow, but don't call before ten."

Bree shook her head. "Went well? Not exactly." She glanced at the time. It was barely eight o'clock.

She made her bed before doing anything else. No one would ever accuse her of being a clean freak, but knowing her bed sat unmade would be something that drove her crazy all day. It was easier to just do it right when she climbed out of it.

She grabbed her fuzzy purple bathrobe from the hook on her closet door and shuffled into the living room of her apartment. Saturday mornings consisted of cold cereal in front of the television while catching up on shows she missed during the week through her DVR.

In her tiny but cozy kitchen, she poured herself a bowl of sugary cereal and doused it in milk from a carton in the fridge. She shuffled back to the living room and turned on the TV. Just as she got comfortable under a plush blanket, cereal bowl in her lap, a loud knock sounded on the door. *No one ever comes to my door, and especially not this early in the morning.*

"If I just sit here, they'll go away," she whispered to herself. "It's probably just a salesman." Thankfully, she hadn't yet opened the blinds on the one window she had facing the outdoor balcony. No one would be able to look in and know she secretly sat on the couch.

Another knock came and again she ignored it,

purposely breathing quietly, as if whoever stood on the other side of the door could actually hear her. By the time the third knock came, curiosity won over her desire to be left alone on her weekend morning. She set the bowl of cereal on the coffee table in front of her and tossed the blanket aside. She tiptoed to the door.

"I know you're in there. I can hear the TV," a voice called as she neared the door.

Bree pressed her eye to the peephole and peered out. Landon stood outside her door, a giant grin on his face. He leaned closer to the door and waved. She jumped back in surprise.

"I saw your eye," he called. "Let me in."

With a sigh, she unlocked the deadbolt but left the chain on. "What are you doing here?"

"I came to observe you, remember? We made a deal."

"You were serious?"

"You knew I was."

Bree brushed a hand across her matted hair. "You never said what time you'd be here."

"I wanted to catch you in your normal environment, before you had a chance to change anything. Now that I'm here, you have to let me in."

"Can't you come back in an hour? I haven't even showered yet." She glanced over her shoulder at the semi-cluttered apartment. "I promise not to change anything."

"Nope. That's not how it works. I'm here to observe, not judge." He lifted his hand into her view and showed that he held a bag from a local bakery. The smells coming from the sack were too enticing to

41

pass up.

With a roll of her eyes, she took the chain off the door and let him in. "Welcome to my humble home."

Landon stepped across the threshold and looked around approvingly. "It's nice. I like it. I've heard good things about this complex."

"It's been good to me." Bree ran her fingers through her hair self-consciously and pulled her bathrobe tighter around her waist, stealing a peek at herself in the mirror on the wall near the front door. She almost gasped out loud when she saw the remnants of last night's makeup smeared underneath her eyes. She licked her finger and rubbed at her eyes, turning around to see Landon watching her with a sideway smile.

She ducked in embarrassment. "I'm going to take a shower. Make yourself at home. The remote's on the coffee table. And before you even ask, the answer is no. You may not observe me in the shower."

For the first time, she managed to trip Landon up. His mouth dropped open and he sunk back against the cushions of her couch. "I wouldn't dream of it," he stammered. "I mean ... uhh ... I'll just wait here for you."

"Good answer."

Bree returned to her bedroom and stared at the pile of clothes thrown on the armchair under the window. After getting home the night before, she didn't have the energy to return all the clothes she'd pulled from their hangers in an attempt to find the 'perfect' outfit. She didn't want to leave Landon alone for too long, not completely trusting him, so she stuffed the pile of clothes in the bottom of her closet, knowing she'd have to iron and maybe even rewash many of them later. *It can't be helped. I don't have any other options.*

Before shutting the closet door, she grabbed another pair of jeans and a green button up shirt from the pile and tucked them under her arm. *Now would be a good time to have a bathroom attached to my bedroom.* She slipped out her door and into the bathroom across the hall, briefly glancing in the direction of the living room. Landon still sat on the couch and didn't look up at the sound of the door.

The warm water of an inviting shower usually soothed her. Staying too long under the stream of the showerhead was one of her guilty pleasures. But that day, knowing a man she barely knew sat on her living room couch took the fun out of the shower. She shampooed her hair, conditioned it, and scrubbed everything else in record time. After dressing, she applied the bare minimum of makeup and twisted her wet hair into a knot on the top of her head.

She started to open the door, but then stopped, returning for a spritz of her favorite perfume. *What are you doing? Don't encourage him! He'll never go away! Wait ... do I want him to go away or not?* She stood with her hand on the bathroom doorknob for a full minute, trying to come to terms with her mixed feelings before taking a deep breath and throwing the door open.

"That was quick," Landon said as she came down the hallway toward him. "I figured I wouldn't see you for another hour."

Bree narrowed her eyes at him. "Are you saying I'm high maintenance?"

Landon put his arms up in defense. "Relax. I'm just used to my sisters. They took forever in the bathroom growing up. That's why I'm an early riser. If I didn't get my turn in the bathroom before six thirty, I wouldn't have another chance until ten."

Bree stepped into her tiny kitchen and leaned against the table. "You have sisters?"

"Two older and one younger."

"Sounds like a full house."

"How about you? Any siblings?" Landon asked.

"Nope. Just me." She fingered the leaves of the houseplant on the table. "I think my parents would have liked to have more, but it never happened for them."

"I can't imagine being an only child."

Bree suddenly laughed and then quickly pursed her lips, trying to cover up her outburst.

A slow smile spread across Landon's face and he took a couple steps toward her in the kitchen. "I'm missing something. Why is that funny?"

"It's not. It's just that ... well ... during Leslie's lecture on what I was allowed to talk about on our date last night, she mentioned family. If I'd only remembered that, you might not be here right now, 'observing me,'" Bree said, making air quotes with her last words.

Landon returned to the living room and sat on the sofa. "Bree, if you're not comfortable doing this, we don't have to," he said. "It's all fun and games. At least, I thought it was. Please don't think that I think of this as a job. I'm sure I came off wrong in the heat of the moment last night. Honestly, I just thought it would be fun to spend the weekend with you and try to prove to you that you don't need make-believe luck to be happy."

Bree sat next to him. "Right. And I agreed to spend the weekend with you because I want to prove to you that you're wrong. Some people have all the luck and some people, namely me, don't." She leaned back against the couch cushions. "That's the way the cards fall, or the way the cookie crumbles, or ... I can't think of any other metaphors."

"Good. I'm glad we're on the same page. Let's make this fun instead of a chore."

"What did you have in mind?"

Landon shrugged. "What do you usually do on Saturday mornings?"

"I usually sit in my bathrobe and catch up on TV I've missed during the week." She glanced at her soggy bowl of cereal still sitting on the coffee table. "And I eat breakfast while I'm doing it."

Landon jumped up. "Right. I brought breakfast. The muffins at the bakery on the corner by my place are to die for." He opened the bag he'd brought with him and produced two blueberry muffins followed by a drink holder containing two plastic cups with the bakery's logo emblazoned on the sides. "I got smoothies, too. Do you want Pineapple Paradise or Strawberry Sensations?"

Bree tapped a finger on her chin. Both sounded good. "Pineapple," she finally answered.

"Good choice." Landon sat back down on the couch next to her. "What are we going to watch?"

"I'm not sure. What kind of shows do you like?"

"Let's just watch whatever you were planning on watching before I interrupted your morning."

Bree lifted the remote hesitantly. *Do I admit that I intended to watch sappy dramas that are probably meant for teenage girls and not twenty-somethings who can't quite let go of their childhood habits?* She punched a couple of buttons on her remote and the contents of her DVR popped up. She let out a breath of relief when she remembered that she'd recorded a documentary about the upcoming St. Patrick's Day holiday. "How about this?" she asked.

Landon smiled halfway. "You really are Irish, aren't you?"

"Is that a no or a yes?"

"I guess it's a yes. To be honest, I've never had a clue why we celebrate St. Patrick's Day, especially here in the states."

"You don't know St. Patrick's story?" Bree opened her mouth in shock. Mama Donovan had pounded the story into her brain her entire life. She assumed everyone knew it.

"Sorry." Landon frowned.

"St. Patrick is the patron saint of Ireland."

Landon smiled sheepishly. "I knew that much."

"Of course, but do you know why?"

"Not a clue."

"Make yourself cozy and I'll tell you," Bree instructed.

Landon grabbed the blanket she'd discarded earlier and piled it onto his lap. "Ready." He tried to look serious, but the corners of his lips twitched.

"Back in the fifth century, St. Patrick was born in Britain. When he was a teenager, somewhere between the age of fourteen and sixteen, he was kidnapped by the Irish."

"Wait … what? The Irish are the bad guys in this story?"

"Be patient. I'm getting there," Bree said. "Back then, the Irish were a pagan people. It was Irish pirates that grabbed St. Patrick and forced him onto their ship. They took him back to their homeland and forced him to work as a slave for six years before he found a way to escape. He found passage on a ship back to his home. When he arrived, he decided to join the clergy. During his studies, he felt like a voice kept telling him he needed to return to Ireland. He had torn feelings about the idea, of course. But, he obeyed what he felt was his call to be a missionary in Ireland and after many years away, he returned. He started teaching the pagan people and built churches all over Ireland as they converted to Christianity. St. Patrick's Day, March 17th, is believed to be the day St. Patrick died." Bree finished her story and sat back, arms folded across her chest.

Landon stared at her with a wide grin.

"What?" she said, feeling more than a little paranoid.

"I found your story very interesting."

She narrowed her eyes. "Are you mocking me?"

Landon shook his head. "Not at all. It really was interesting. But it also showed that you're passionate about things other than superstitions. You came alive just now. I liked it."

"Thanks … I think." Bree cleared her throat. "So do you want to watch the documentary now?"

"Do we need to? I think you told me everything."

"Good point." She scanned the list of shows again and then turned the TV off. "I'm not really in the mood to watch anything. Let's do something else."

"I came up with a few ideas last night."

"Such as?"

"We're going to make you break all the rules of good luck, starting with this." He pulled a tiny mirror from his back pocket. "You have to break it so I can prove to you that you won't have seven years of bad luck as the saying goes."

Bree closed her eyes and groaned. It was going to be a looong weekend.

# Chapter 6

**B**ree stared at the little mirror Landon held in his hands. Her heart rate increased just thinking about the bad things that would happen to her if she went along with Landon's plans. A weekend might only be two days long, but she could amass a lifetime of bad luck in two days time if Landon insisted on her breaking all her superstitious rules.

She shook her head. "I'm not breaking that."

"Come on, Bree. You agreed to my plan. You can't back out now."

"Sure I can."

"Think through this logically. Do you honestly believe that breaking a mirror will give you seven years of bad luck?"

"Yes, I do. In seventh grade, I slammed my locker door shut. The magnetic mirror I had on the inside of the door fell down and shattered. You can't even imagine the bad things that happened after that."

Landon raised his eyebrows. "Such as?"

"I don't know, all kinds of stuff."

"You can't even name anything."

Bree frowned. "I started struggling on school tests, I didn't win the student council election at the end of the year, my pet hamster died."

"What proof do you have that those things happened because of a locker mishap? I'm not sure if you're aware of it or not, but bad things happen to people all the time."

"Right. It's because they've cursed themselves."

"I got the new car I have now because some idiot ran a red light and totaled my other one. It's been a month but I still have occasional neck pain from it. Are you suggesting I did something to deserve it?" Landon asked.

"Absolutely." Bree nodded. "I only met you yesterday, though, so I can't begin to guess at what you did."

Landon laughed. "The more I talk to you, the more I'm convinced this isn't just a game."

Bree glared. "You think this is a game? This is my real life—my reality."

He put his hands up. "Okay. I'm sorry. I've kind of assumed you were messing with me, but I now realize you're serious about these matters. I'll try to be nicer."

"Thank you."

"Now," he handed her the tiny mirror, "it's time to break this."

Bree took the mirror with trembling fingers. "I guess if I'm going to die on Sunday anyway, it doesn't matter if I have seven years of bad luck, right?"

"Way to be positive. We're off to a great start."

*I can't believe I'm about to do this. He just doesn't*

*understand. He's been blessed with good looks, a great job, and confidence. I don't have any of those things. If I just hadn't lost my Irish luck ...* Bree closed her eyes, took a deep breath, and dropped the mirror on her coffee table. She waited for hellfire to rain down, but nothing happened. She cautiously opened her eyes. Landon sat, holding the mirror out to her again.

"It didn't break," he said. "Try it again."

"Maybe the kitchen floor will work better. It will be easier to sweep up anyway." Bree took the mirror again and marched into her kitchen. The floor space was small, but it had real tiles. Bree dropped the mirror again. That time it didn't shatter, but it did break in half. Bree shivered as she looked at the two pieces on the floor.

"Great job," Landon said, coming up behind her and patting her on the back. "I knew you could do it. And nothing bad happened."

"Yet."

He bent down to pick up the broken pieces. "Ouch!"

"What's wrong?"

Landon stood and held up a finger already dripping in blood. "Got a bandage?"

"How did you manage to do that?" Bree cried as she grabbed for a napkin off the counter. "Hold your hand up," she instructed as she wrapped the napkin around his finger.

"Thanks," Landon whispered.

Bree tilted her head and looked at him. "Are you okay? You look really pale."

He slowly moved his head back and forth. "Blood. I don't like blood."

"Oh goodness, come sit down. I don't want you passing out on the kitchen floor or you'll have more than a cut finger." She helped him to the couch and instructed him to lie down while she ran to the bathroom to get a bandage. Considering the size of the mirror, she couldn't believe how deep the cut was. Any deeper and she would have recommended stitches. "There you go," she said as she finished securing tape around the gauze. "No more blood ... at least, not that you can see."

"You probably think I'm a child," Landon said as some of the color returned to his face.

"Trust me, as a nurse I've seen my fair share of people who don't do blood. I've seen adults who had to be physically restrained just to get their finger pricked."

Landon grinned and sat up. "I thought I'd outgrow this, but I haven't. Maybe when I'm thirty."

"Maybe."

"Okay. First test is done and you don't have any signs of bad luck yet."

Bree shook her head and pointed to the kitchen. "Wrong. You just bled on my kitchen floor. That's a sign of bad luck."

Landon rolled his eyes. "I disagree. It's a normal coincidence. Now, I have an idea for the next test, but we'll have to leave your apartment."

Bree eyed him suspiciously. "Where are we going?"

"You'll see. It's not far."

She slipped her shoes on and grabbed the jacket she'd draped over a kitchen chair after arriving home the night before. She patted her pockets, but couldn't find what she was looking for. "Hold on. I'll be right back." She hurried down the small hallway to her bedroom and sifted through the contents on her bedside table. It wasn't there.

Next, she opened the closet and dug for the clothes she'd worn the night before amongst the pile she'd tossed in earlier. After feeling all the pockets in the jeans she gave up and emerged from the closet, slightly more disheveled than when she went in. "Maybe it fell out in the bathroom," she whispered to herself.

Across the hall, she searched the floor behind the toilet, around the shower, and under the sink. It was gone. Her good luck charm had vanished. With defeat, she turned around, gasping when she saw Landon standing in the doorway of the bathroom.

"Looking for something?" he said.

"Yes."

"Can I help?"

"It's ... no." The last thing she needed during her moment of crisis was another lecture from Landon Murray about the reality of luck.

She stepped toward the doorway, planning on exiting, but Landon didn't budge. Instead, he grinned and reached into his pocket. "Is this what you're looking for?" he asked as he dangled her lucky rabbit's foot in front of her face.

Bree grabbed it from him. "Where did you find it?"

"On the seat of my car. You must have dropped it in your rush to get away from me last night." He stepped aside so she could leave the bathroom. "And, judging by how much fur has been rubbed off by excessive handling, I figured you'd miss it."

"Thanks," she said sheepishly.

"My pleasure. Now, can we go try my next experiment?"

"Lead the way."

Outside the apartment, Bree breathed in deeply, enjoying the spring weather and scents. Daffodils and tulips bloomed around her complex and she couldn't get enough of the colors of their bobbing heads.

Much to Bree's surprise, Landon took her hand and led her down the sidewalk, away from the parking lot where she could clearly see his car. "Where are we going?"

"I saw something as I pulled in this morning that we could use in our experiments."

As they rounded the corner of her building and she saw what lay ahead, Bree stopped in her tracks. "Uh uh. No way. Never in my life have I done that."

Landon stood in front of her and took her other hand, pulling her toward him. He leaned down so their faces were only inches apart and she felt herself melting ... just a little. *Careful Bree, the devil is using his charm to ... to ... Ah, dang. He smells sooo good.*

"If it makes you feel better, I'll go first," he whispered.

Bree looked over his shoulder in the direction they were headed. A ladder, left by men who'd been working on the rain gutters that week, stood open at the edge of the sidewalk. "Fine," she said with a small nod.

Landon grinned. "That was easier than I expected. I figured you'd bolt and I'd have to chase you, not that I wouldn't have enjoyed that."

Bree tried to hide her smile, unsuccessfully, as he

pulled her toward the ladder. The closer they got the more she squeezed his hand. Her other hand squeezed the rabbit's foot inside her pocket.

"Ready?" he said.

"No."

"Good." He stepped under the ladder and pulled her with him. She assumed he'd continue through to the other side, but he stopped under it and wrapped his arms around her so she couldn't go anywhere. "See. It's nice under here. And cozy."

Her heart picked up its pace. She couldn't quite decipher the feeling. *Is my heart going crazy from fear or physical contact with Landon?* She tried to wiggle out of his grasp, but he held her tight. "You're mean."

Landon laughed. "I know. I'm sorry." He let go of her and stepped out from under the ladder. Just as he emerged, a gust of wind kicked up. A small flower pot sitting on the apartment balcony above him blew down, hitting him on the forehead and knocking him to the ground.

"Oh no!" Bree cried as she knelt next to him on the ground. "Are you okay?"

Landon sat up and gingerly touched his head. "That's going to leave a bump. Am I bleeding again?"

Bree ran her fingers through his hair, checking for any cuts. She pulled back when she saw him grinning at her. "No. You'll live."

"That came out of nowhere," he said.

"That's what *you* think."

"You know something I don't know?"

Bree pursed her lips. "It's because you walked under the stupid ladder. Whoever it is that pulls the strings of fate and luck is probably sitting on a cloud laughing at you right now."

"It could have happened to anyone."

"But it didn't. It happened to the guy who walked under a ladder."

Landon shook his head and sighed. "Fine. We'll agree to disagree on this one, too. The next experiment is a simple one and in no way will it make either one of us get hurt or have a bazillion years of bad luck."

Landon stood and offered a hand to pull Bree up. She brushed the remnants of potting soil from her knees while he shook it out of his hair and shirt. *He looks kind of cute with his hair out of place. Stop, Bree ... he's the devil, remember? He's making you go against all your traditions. Mama Donovan would be so disappointed.*

"Why are you glaring at me?" Landon said, interrupting her thoughts.

Bree raised her eyebrows. "I'm not glaring. I was just thinking."

"You're a pretty intense thinker."

"You could say that. Where's the next test?"

Landon stepped back onto the sidewalk. "Right here."

"We're doing the whole ladder thing again? It didn't go so well the first time," Bree said with a mocking smile.

Landon pointed at the sidewalk. "I'm going to convince you that it's okay to step on the cracks."

Admittedly, stepping on a crack didn't concern Bree quite as much as some of the other superstitions. Landon had been right the night before when he said most people outgrew the game. For some reason, she never had. Just one more weird quirk in her quiver. "Step on a crack you break your mother's back," she said. *I wonder how many of my fears are habits rather than superstitions. I wish Mama Donovan were here to talk to.*

Landon grinned. "Ah, yes. That's what the rhyme was. I couldn't quite remember it."

"That parts just a silly rhyme, but I'm sure it really can bring bad luck."

"We'll see."

Landon strolled down the sidewalk ahead of her, purposely stepping on every crack in his way.

Bree strode along behind him, purposely missing all the cracks.

Landon looked over his shoulder. "You're not doing it," he said, turning around and walking backward.

"This is my natural stride. To step on a crack, I'd have to break it. That's just ridiculous."

"No excuses. Do it, Bree."

She sighed and stopped mid stride. Then, she carefully set her foot down right on one of the cracks. "Does that make you happy?"

"Actually, it—"

Bree gasped as she watched Landon tumble off the sidewalk and onto the pavement of the parking lot. "Are you okay?"

Landon sat up. "I guess that's why Mom always told me not to walk backward."

Bree shook her head back and forth and struggled to keep from laughing. "I don't even have a response for this." She reached down and offered a hand to Landon. He winced when he put pressure on his ankle. "You're hurt." She didn't bother to mention the scrape on the back of his elbow.

"No I'm not. I can walk it off." From deep within his pocket, his cell phone began to ring. He pulled it out and looked at the screen. Concern flashed in his eyes. "It's my mom. I hope her back is okay."

Bree's hands flew to her mouth and she let out a little moan.

Landon, seeing her reaction, put a hand on her shoulder. "Sorry. That was mean. It's my office, not my mom." He grinned. "I thought you'd laugh."

Bree slugged him in the chest. "Jerk."

"This will just be a minute." He held up one finger and stepped away to answer the phone call.

Bree wandered over to a patch of clover growing amid the grass of the common area and sat down. She couldn't pass up the opportunity to look for a four-leaf clover. She'd looked through countless patches of clover in her lifetime, but never found the elusive anomaly. Carrying a four-leaf clover around would be the ultimate in good luck charms.

Bree wasn't sure how long she sat in the patch, but it must have been a while because her eyes started to droop and she lay back in the grass. She didn't hear Landon arrive, but his familiar scent entered her nose and she opened her eyes to see him kneeling over her.

"That took a lot longer than I thought. I'm sorry," he said.

"No problem."

"I know I told you I'd spend the entire weekend with you, but there's a bit of an emergency at work. I can't even tell you the last time I had to go in on a Saturday. In fact, I don't think I've *ever* had to.

Hopefully it won't take long, but I don't have a choice."

"I understand. Things happen." *Usually after you've been messing with bad luck.*

"I'll call you as soon as I finish and we'll pick up where we left off. Deal?"

Bree stretched her arms over her head in the clover. "Deal."

Landon started to lean toward her, but then stopped and stood. "See ya."

As Bree sat up and watched him drive away, she frowned. *I'm in worse trouble than I thought. I'm falling for the devil.*

# Chapter 7

**B**ack inside her apartment, Bree kicked off her shoes and looked around. The morning had filled her with energy, and the idea of sitting back on the couch and watching TV no longer appealed to her. With an unusual vigor, she emptied her dishwasher, vacuumed the living room carpet, sponge-mopped the small kitchen floor, and watered all eight of her houseplants scattered through the living area.

In her bedroom, she neatly hung all her clothing back on the hangers and organized them in the closet according to long-sleeves and short-sleeves. The jeans were lined up according to shade of blue and her slacks placed next to them. Opening her dresser, she refolded all her scrubs and arranged them in a way that would make it easier to rotate.

Looking around at everything she accomplished, she nodded her head and smiled. "Not bad for a Saturday morning. Maybe I should do things like this more often."

She wondered if she should wait for Landon to return to eat lunch, but it was already one and she'd burned a lot of energy cleaning. When her stomach growled, it was the last straw. In the kitchen, Bree grabbed a can of chicken and vegetable noodle soup from the cupboard and popped the top off, pouring it into a pan on the stove. Her eyes drifted to the door and then to her phone, making sure it still had a charge.

She tried to decipher her feelings as she slowly sipped the soup. *Am I more anxious for Landon to get back because I miss him or because I'm worried that his actions this morning have caused some catastrophic event to happen to him? What if he cursed himself so much, he got into a horrific accident on Harrison Boulevard?* The more she thought about it, the more the fear sunk in.

When her cell phone rang, she leaped to grab it off the kitchen counter. "Landon," she whispered as she answered it without looking at the screen. "Hello?" she said eagerly.

*"Whoa. You're bright and cheery this morning."*

Leslie. Not Landon.

"I'm cleaning my apartment," Bree responded.

*"And that's making you happy? It usually puts you in a bad mood."*

Bree shrugged even though she knew Leslie couldn't see the gesture through the phone. "It's springtime. Spring makes me happy."

*"Spring doesn't officially start for another week. Is it the weather or is it a particular guy you went out with last night?"*

Bree sunk back in her chair. "It's definitely the weather."

"*You never called me last night.*"

"Sorry. I got in late."

"*How late?*"

"Why does that matter?"

"*The later you get home, the better the date went.*"

"I think it was about 9:30."

Silence filled the other end of the line. "*Are you messing with me?*"

"No."

"*Oh, Bree. I'm sorry it didn't go well. What happened? Did you forget what I told you and talk about superstitions?*"

"Our conversations were doomed right from the start. He was in the room when Florence predicted my death."

"*You're still thinking about that?*"

"A little."

"*Was he at least nice about it?*"

Bree took a moment to think about that question. "Well, sort of. He's a polite guy. He just doesn't believe in luck."

"*So ... you're saying he's normal?*"

"I'm saying we have different opinions on things. This morning he made me break a mirror, walk under a ladder, and step on a crack in the sidewalk."

Leslie laughed through the phone and then suddenly stopped. "*Wait ... what? This morning? Are you with him right now?*"

"No. He left."

"*But he was there. Bree! This is awesome! You might have found the only guy in the world who doesn't run away because of your fears."*

"I'm just an experiment to him. He's an efficiency consultant. He observes people and then recommends change. I'm nothing more than a project to him. He even called me that to my face last night."

*"And you agreed to this?"*

Bree tried to remind herself why she let Landon talk her into his crazy scheme. "He's really cute. And he smells good."

Leslie sighed. *"Honey, you really need to get out more. I promise to be better about setting you up with guys. Now that you've gone on one blind date, maybe I can get you to agree to others."*

"We'll see." Bree's phone beeped and she pulled it away from her ear to look at the caller ID. "I've got to go. Landon's calling."

*"Don't let him treat you like crap."*

"Trust me, with the amount of bad luck he's brought upon himself, it's me that's having the most fun."

Bree hung up with Leslie and quickly changed back to Landon. "Hello?"

*"I was wrong. The problem at work took far longer than expected."*

"No problem. I got a lot done around here."

*"Ready to go again?"*

"That probably depends on what you had in mind."

*"I'm standing outside your door. Let me in and I'll tell you."*

Bree jumped up from the table and rushed down the hall to the bathroom. "Be right there," she said into the phone as she took down the earlier knot she'd tied on top of her head and finger-combed her hair. She added another spritz of perfume before opening the door.

Bree took one look at Landon and her jaw dropped. "What happened to you?"

Landon's white t-shirt was covered in brown stains. "As I was coming out of the elevator at work, an overly eager intern rushed in with drinks for the management team. She ran into me and I got the raw end of the deal."

Bree tried to stop herself from laughing, but she couldn't.

"Stop that," Landon insisted as Bree flopped onto the couch, doubling-over in fits of laughter.

"I can't," she managed to say between giggles. "I thought I had the world's worst luck, but I don't. *You* do." More laughter.

"Things happen."

"All in one morning?"

Landon lifted his shoulders and dropped them. "Sometimes." He held up his hand, indicating another shirt. "I always keep a change of clothes in my trunk. Mind if I use your bathroom to change?"

"Be my guest."

When Landon emerged from the bathroom twelve point two seconds later, Bree wished he would have stayed in the dirty shirt. She'd already been struggling not to flirt with him or fall for him, but seeing him in the tighter black t-shirt that showed off his toned body would make him even harder to resist. It wouldn't be a problem, except that he was in the 'relationship' for different reasons than her. The last thing she wanted to deal with at the end of the weekend was heartbreak.

Landon held up the dirty shirt. "Do you have any stain remover I could put on this?"

Bree pointed at the closet next to the bathroom. "The washer and dryer are in there. Stain remover is on top next to the detergent." She could have gotten up and showed him herself, but she didn't dare get too close to him while he wore *that* shirt.

"Thanks."

"What devilish things do you have in mind for me next?" she called down the hall.

"Actually, I thought you could have a turn. There are things you say cause bad luck and things that inspire good luck. Maybe we could try some of the good luck things now."

Bree sat up and leaned forward. "I like that idea. Much less stressful on my part. Did you have something specific in mind?"

He returned to the living room. "That's for you to decide. I'm not as versed in the subject as you."

"We could start with the clover patch outside. I've always wanted to find a four-leaf clover."

Landon tilted his head and looked at her. "Is that what you were doing when you were lying there earlier today?"

"I didn't find anything."

"Maybe we'll have better *luck*," he emphasized the word, "this time."

"No mocking."

"Sorry."

Back outside, the pair sat in the patch of clover and sifted through the plant. By that time of day, people were headed out and about and they got more than one odd look from curious passersby. Landon didn't seem to notice as he dug through the clover.

"This doesn't embarrass you?" Bree asked after the fifth strange look.

"Sitting in a bed of clover with a pretty girl would never be embarrassing," Landon quipped.

"Good answer. Find anything yet?"

"Nope. Why clover anyway?" he asked.

"What do you mean?"

"What's the legend behind it? Why does it supposedly bring good luck?"

Bree raised her eyebrows. "I didn't get to that part about St. Patrick this morning, did I? Maybe we should have watched the documentary after all. It's still on the DVR you know."

Landon stretched his legs out in front of himself. "I prefer hearing your voice over some boring narrator. I trust you to explain it to me correctly."

"There's not that much to tell, really. When St. Patrick returned to Ireland to convert the pagans to Christianity, he used clover to teach about the Holy Trinity. Each leaf of the clover represented a different being. One for God, one for His son, and one for the Holy Spirit."

"That makes sense, but who was the fourth leaf for?" Landon asked.

"Good question. Actually, St. Patrick used a normal three-leaf clover or a shamrock. The Irish use a three-leaf clover as their symbol. Four leaf clovers are just for luck."

"I see. Any other Irish things I need to know about?"

"I could spend the entire day telling you things."

"Your grandmother ... what did you call her?"

"Mama Donovan."

He twirled a piece of clover in his fingers. "Right. Mama Donovan. She must have really cared about her culture if she taught you to be so passionate about it."

"She always dreamed of returning to her homeland. She was happy here, I know that, but once her husband—my grandpa—died and she moved in with my parents, her reasons to return to Ireland started to outweigh her reasons to stay."

"Have you ever been there?"

"To Ireland?"

Landon nodded.

Bree frowned and shook her head. "We were planning a family trip there a few years ago, but that's when Mama Donovan's health started to deteriorate and she never felt up to traveling. When she died, the trip died with her. I'd still love to make it there someday."

"It's a beautiful place."

Bree quickly sat up and stared at Landon. "You've been there?"

He nodded slowly.

"And you're just barely telling me this now?"

"I've been to a lot of places." He tossed the clover he'd been playing with across the grass. "Besides, I've barely known you for twenty-four hours. There's probably a lot about me I haven't gotten around to mentioning yet."

Bree tilted her head toward the sky and closed her eyes, letting the sun warm her face. "I can't believe you went there and didn't even learn about St. Patrick."

"To be fair, I was only thirteen. Dad was going on business and took the family to tag along. He did that sometimes. Since he spent most of the time in meetings, we didn't have a lot of time to explore."

"What was it like?"

"Very green, as I'm sure you can imagine. Definitely not like Utah."

"What else?"

"Hmm ... I remember the fairy mounds."

Bree snorted and opened her eyes. "Please tell me you don't believe any of that fairy nonsense."

Landon leaned closer to her and put a hand on her knee. "Wait ... are you saying there's something you *don't* believe in?"

She stared at his hand. "Think about it. Little people with wings that go around causing mischief? It's ridiculous."

Landon dropped his head into his hands and shook it back and forth. "I'm at a loss for words."

"Why?"

"How can someone who believes that walking under a ladder will curse her with bad luck not believe in fairies?"

"Grandma Donovan said—"

"Ah hah!" He pointed at Bree. "I knew it had something to do with that woman."

"She was a smart woman. She had her priorities straight."

"You're such a mystery."

Bree sighed and stood up. "I think we've exhausted this patch of clover. If there was a four-leafer here, we would have found it by now."

Landon followed suit and stood, brushing the

grass from his backside. "It's still your turn. What else can we do that will bring us good luck?"

Bree scrunched up her face, thinking hard. She snapped her fingers. "I've got it. We'll need to go to Walmart or the mall or somewhere with a really big parking lot."

Landon raised his eyebrows. "I'm intrigued. And I'm beginning to realize there's never a dull moment when you're involved."

# Chapter 8

Fifteen minutes later, Landon turned into the parking lot of the local Walmart and headed for a parking stall near the front of the store. Bree reached over and put her hand on his arm. "Wait!"

Landon turned to her with questioning eyes.

"Park in the back. We're not actually going inside."

Landon shook his head in amusement, but obeyed. "This just keeps getting better."

"We've got to counteract all the bad luck you brought upon yourself and forced on me this morning."

"And how are we going to do that?" he asked as he parked in the last space of the huge parking area. At least a dozen empty spaces filled the gap between Landon's car and the next vehicle.

"When you were a kid, and maybe as an adult, didn't you pick up coins when you saw them on the ground?"

"Of course."

"And how does the saying go?" Bree prompted.

Landon nodded slowly. "I see where this is going. If I remember correctly, it went something like … find a penny, pick it up, all day long you'll have good luck."

"Exactly. But remember, if the coin is heads up, feel free to take it. If it's facing down, just pretend you never saw it."

"If I leave it there, isn't that a form of littering?"

"Not unless you're the one that dropped the coin in the first place."

"But isn't it my civic duty to help keep our community clean?"

"Trust me, there are plenty of other people out there who can pick it up. It doesn't have to be you."

Landon scanned the parking lot. "Are we searching this entire area?"

"Why not?"

"I'm not against it, I just think if we're going to cover this much area, we should make it a contest."

Bree raised her eyebrows. "A contest?"

"We split the parking lot in half and each cover an area. Whichever one of us finds the most money wins."

Bree zipped up her jacket and lifted her purse strap around her neck. "I like that. What do we win?"

"Loser buys ice cream."

"Deal," Bree said, sticking her hand out to shake Landon's. He didn't let go immediately and her heart rate sped up a little as the seconds ticked by with her hand still resting in his. She didn't want to let go, but...

"Go!" Landon suddenly yelled as he dropped her hand and sprinted to his half of the parking lot.

Bree hurried to her side, only instead of running around haphazardly like Landon, she thought of the

71

parking lot like a grid and began her search in the back corner. Up and down, back and forth, she walked. Head down, shoulders hunched. Every time she neared the front of the store, where the majority of the people were, some well-meaning person would stop to ask her if they could help her find her missing item. They all assumed she'd lost her car keys or a contact lens.

Twenty minutes later, Bree and Landon met up in the middle of the parking lot. "Well," Bree said. "Any luck? And yes, I mean luck."

"You first," he said.

Bree lifted a fist toward him and then turned her hand over, opening her palm. "One quarter, two dimes, and six pennies. I also left three nickels and two pennies on the ground because they were tails up. I believe my total is fifty-one cents."

"Not bad. I'm impressed," Landon said with a nod of his head.

"How'd you do?"

Landon reached into his pocket and pulled out a handful of change. "It's $1.28, but you can count it if you don't believe me."

Bree squinted at him. "I don't believe you. You had that spare change in your pocket all along.

"Nope."

"You begged for change in front of the store."

"Nope."

"You broke into a vending machine."

Landon put a hand over her mouth. "Bree, I won. Oh, and I prefer cookies and cream ice cream."

❧

"I still can't believe you found that much money in a parking lot," Bree said as they sat down in a corner booth at a local ice cream parlor. "Maybe that's where I should have gone when I needed extra cash as a kid. Would have saved me time on a lot of boring chores to earn extra allowance."

Landon patted himself on the back, but then his demeanor changed. "Tell me, how much of your superstitions and habits come from your grandma and how many of them are ones you've adopted on your own? I'm pretty sure not all the things you believe in are Irish traditions. In fact, I'd say most of them aren't."

Bree jabbed her spoon into her ice cream a few times, but didn't bring the spoon to her mouth. "I suppose some of them are ones I've adopted myself from other cultures. But, if something works for one culture, why wouldn't it work for another?"

"How well do they really work, though?"

Bree hesitated. *Do I want him to know how I really feel? Sometimes I question my habits ...* "I'll admit, the good luck charms don't always work, but the bad ones do."

A group of teenage boys walked by their table. Bree didn't know what they were discussing, but a lot of high-fiving and backslapping was going on. What happened next seemed to happen in slow motion. She saw it coming, she knew what was going to happen, but she couldn't do anything to stop it.

One particularly boisterous boy slapped another

laughing boy so hard, he lost the grip on his chocolate cone and it tumbled out of his hand, rocketing through the air on a direct path to its destination. It hit Landon square in the chest and slid down the front of his shirt to his pants.

Bree gasped and covered her mouth with her hands, but didn't say anything as she watched Landon stare at the mess in his lap. The noisy boys quieted and stared at the aftermath, waiting for a reaction from Landon. Finally, he raised his head and looked at them.

"Hey man, I'm sorry. It slipped. I swear I didn't do it on purpose," the red-faced owner of the cone said, a pleading look in his eyes.

"Would you mind handing me some napkins?" Landon said through clenched teeth.

Bree bit her lip to keep from laughing as she watched him mop up the mess, knowing he'd brought the accident upon himself after all of his morning shenanigans. *I just don't understand why the same bad things aren't happening to me? I did everything he did.*

"Maybe we better call it a day. I only had one spare shirt in my trunk," Landon said as they climbed into his car to leave a few minutes later. His black shirt didn't look too bad, but chocolate ice cream smeared all over the front of his jeans elicited more than one strange look as they walked to his car.

"You're probably right," Bree agreed, still trying not to laugh at him.

They drove in silence for the first few minutes, but Landon turned to her at a stoplight. "Go ahead and say it. I know you're dying to."

Bree tilted her head at him. "I don't know what

74

you're talking about."

"You wanted to prove me wrong this entire day, and you're dying to tell me I told you so," he said. "You're convinced that this happened to me because I'm cursed. I made you break a mirror, I picked up the money wrong, I stepped on the cracks, I walked under a ladder. Am I right?"

Bree gave him a half smile. "I would never kick you while you're down ... wait a second. What was that part about the money?"

Landon turned away, not looking her in the eyes. "Did I say that part out loud?"

Bree gasped. "That's how you got so much money! You picked up coins that were tails up, didn't you?"

Landon cleared his throat. "Guilty."

Bree shook her head. "A liar and a cheater."

Landon shook his head as he pulled into the parking lot of her apartment complex. "I never lied about it. In my defense, you didn't specifically ask me which way all the coins were facing. So, I'm only a cheater."

Bree wiped a hand across her forehead. "Phew. That makes me feel so much better." She reached for the handle on the door, but stopped when Landon put a hand on her arm.

"Are we still on for tomorrow? I promise not to distract you while you're working. You'll barely know I'm there and it will be good for me to spend some time with my grandma. I'm not done with this project yet."

Bree suppressed a frown. "Of course. A deal is a deal."

Inside her apartment, she kicked off her shoes and

flopped onto her couch. All the energy she'd gained by cleaning earlier in the day had been zapped from her. In her mood, she could barely muster the energy to watch TV. Landon's first shirt, the one the intern spilled the drinks on, still sat on the coffee table. Her fingers brushed it as she reached for the remote. She picked it up and a bit of his scent drifted into her nose. With a gasp, she dropped the shirt and scooted to the other end of the couch.

"Don't go there, Bree. No matter how cute he is, or how fun it is to hang out with him, he even said it himself. You're only a project to him," she whispered.

# Chapter 9

"Ah hah!" Leslie cried when Bree stepped behind the nurse's station on Sunday morning. "The prodigal daughter has returned."

"I never left," Bree said as she squeezed her friend's shoulder with one arm.

"Maybe not, but you weren't answering texts or calls. What's a girl to do when her best friend suddenly goes phone silent?"

"I had a busy day yesterday. Sorry."

"Sorry? That's all you have to say?" Leslie grinned. "What were you and Landon doing that you didn't have a spare minute to call? And don't tell me you weren't with him because I won't believe you."

"He came back after you and I talked and we hung out a little more. That's all."

Leslie sat down in a chair next to the computer and began to spin around. "I knew it was fate when Jason suggested setting you up."

"It's not fate. I'm his project, remember? After

today, I doubt he'll ever call me again."

"Today?"

Bree pulled Leslie out of the spinning chair and took her place at the computer so she could clock in. "He's coming by to visit Florence ... his grandmother. Since she's my patient, I'm sure I'll see him. He mentioned he'd like to observe me, whatever that means."

Leslie leaned closer to Bree. "Sounds kinky."

Bree glared at her. "It's just proof that he in no way wants to continue seeing me in a normal way. I'm a game that will all be over after today. Besides that, it's March 15th. I could be dead by the end of the day and it won't matter anyway."

Leslie leaned back against the wall and sighed. "Stop talking like that. You're making me depressed. Jason told me last night about plans for a romantic date next weekend and I should be happy today."

Bree's eyes lit up. "You're going to get engaged."

Leslie tried not to smile, but she couldn't hold it back. "You think so? I wondered, but I don't want to get my hopes up. Wouldn't it be nice, though?"

Bree reached up and hugged her friend. "Trust me, that's his intent. And if for some reason it's not, you'll still get a romantic date and the ring and question will soon be on their way."

"I hope so. I really feel like he's the one."

"Oh, he's definitely the one."

"Who's the one? Me?" a male voice said, approaching them from behind.

Bree felt herself blush as she sat up straighter in her chair. Landon Murray leaned against the counter.

"Hi, Landon. Good to see you again," Leslie said

before excusing herself to go check on patients.

Landon turned to Bree. "I didn't mean to chase her away."

"You didn't. She really does need to check on her patients."

"Who were you two talking about?"

"That's none of your business."

"I figure it was either me or Jason. Am I right?" His eyes twinkled.

"Maybe," Bree said as she raised her shoulders dramatically and then dropped them again.

"That's basically a yes in my book."

Bree crossed her arms over her chest. "Jason better hurry up and propose before she bursts."

"Guys don't talk about things like that with each other very often. I mean, it's just not in the guy code. But, I can say with some degree of confidence, that I think it's coming soon."

"That a vague answer."

"Sorry. It's the best I've got."

Bree stepped around the counter with her clipboard in her hand. Landon looked her up and down and grinned. Suddenly self-conscious, she patted her hair to make sure there weren't an unusual amount of flyaways and rubbed her tongue along her teeth to check for leftover breakfast.

"I like this look on you," Landon said.

Bree looked down at her scrubs. The pants were dark blue and the shirt a light blue with rainbows. Leslie once threatened to draw pots of gold on the shirt when Bree wouldn't break one of her superstitious habits. "You like the tired, frumpy nurse look?" Bree asked.

"I prefer to call it the cute career woman look, but we can go with your description if you'd rather." He reached out and touched the bun on top of Bree's head.

She stepped back, remembering she was only a project and allowing herself to fall for him would only lead to heartbreak. "I need to check on my patients. Why don't I walk you to your grandmother's room?" *And then I'll leave you there so I won't have to keep looking at you.*

"Lead the way," Landon said with a sweep of his arm.

At Florence's door, Bree peeked through the window first. Florence sat up in bed, staring at the TV hanging from the ceiling. Bree tapped on the door and then walked in. "Good morning, Florence. It's good to see you again. I brought a visitor for you."

Florence looked at Bree without any recognition on her face. When Landon stepped out from behind Bree, Florence's face lit up.

"You've returned," Florence gasped. "After all these years. I don't know why you left me alone for so long. Oh well, it's all water under the bridge. Come, sweetheart, sit on the bed by me."

Bree raised her eyebrows and looked at Landon. "You haven't been visiting her?" she said accusingly.

"She thinks I'm her husband ... my grandpa. Everyone tells me I look just like him. He died when I was four," he whispered. He leaned right into her ear and Bree held her breath as his nose brushed her face. "I told you before. She's crazy."

He crossed the room and sat on the bed next to his grandmother. "I'm sorry. I got delayed. You know how things are. What are we going to watch today?"

Florence looked at the clock on the wall next to the TV. "It's nine o'clock. You know what we'll be watching."

"Of course I know. I wasn't aware of the time." Landon looked at Bree and shrugged his shoulders. "*I have absolutely no idea!*" he mouthed. Bree turned away from the two of them to keep from laughing. She quietly went about the room, checking on Florence's vitals and administering her morning medication. She got her a fresh mug of water and made sure the woman was warm enough before leaving.

"See ya around," Landon called as she stepped out of the room.

"I'll be here," she called back.

Out in the hall, she smiled to herself. Many of the patients in her care suffered from memory loss and Alzheimer's, but they were still human and she appreciated the family members who came in anyway and still treated them with kindness. She'd seen way too many patients whose family never came to visit because the patient 'wouldn't know we came anyway.'

Bree spent the next hour completing her first round of checks on her five patients. Mrs. Beth, as Elizabeth Reynolds liked to be called, was the most coherent and lucid of all her patients, but still one of the highest maintenance. Half her body remained paralyzed from a stroke that occurred in her younger years. Arthritis, osteoporosis, and general old age had left her body fragile. But, she never wasted a moment to share a good story from her youth. That morning was no exception and Bree found herself sneaking peeks at her watch after the third tale from the Great

Depression. She finally packed Mrs. Beth into a wheelchair and took her to the common room where she continued her stories to the other patients gathered there. Most of them smiled and nodded along with her tales although Bree knew they could barely remember their own names. The quality of the audience didn't matter as much as the quantity to Mrs. Beth.

Mr. Carlisle, another of her patients, already sat on a couch in the common room, smiling as he observed the others around him. He never said much—he could barely hear anyway—but he always had a smile for anyone and everyone who happened upon him. He never slept much either and spent almost all his hours in the common room. When coming on shift, Bree knew to search him out there before checking his room.

Next, Bree stopped in on Pearl Lerner. Of all the residents at Shady Elms, Pearl was the youngest at sixty-seven and had the fewest visible health problems. But, she held the record for craziest. Her room had to remain locked from the outside at all times or she would bolt. Bree didn't think her runs were an attempt at escaping the nursing home, but more a game of cat and mouse. She rarely ran toward the outer doors and spent most of her time running up and down the halls and in and out of the rooms of other patients, giggling the entire time. It drove cranky Mr. Hansen nuts. Since other patients and visitors didn't appreciate witnessing Pearl being cornered and ushered back to her room, the staff tried to keep her runs to a minimum.

"How are you this morning, Pearl?" Bree asked as

she entered the room.

Pearl jumped up from the chair where she'd been coloring a picture of a clown and headed for the door. Bree quickly pushed it shut with her foot and put her arms on Pearl's shoulders before she could go any farther.

"Pearl wants to run," the gray-haired woman said.

"I know, but Pearl needs to stay in her room a little longer."

"Pearl likes to run. It's fun. People run with me."

"I think they're running after you, hon."

Pearl plopped into her chair and stuck her lip out. "They can't keep up with Pearl."

"Later today, when it's warmer, I'll take you outside into the yard and you can run as much as you'd like."

Pearl bounced in her chair and clapped her hands. Before Bree could stop her, she picked up the red crayon she'd used to fill in the clown's lips and popped it into her mouth. "Pearl doesn't like this candy. It tastes like wax."

"It *is* wax, Pearl." Bree picked up another crayon from the table. "See? You ate one of these."

"Why would Pearl do that? Those aren't food."

Bree lifted the wastebasket to the woman's mouth and Pearl spit the slobbery remnants of the red crayon into it. "I'll put in your favorite movie right now. When it ends in two hours, you can eat lunch and then I'll take you outside. Does that sound like a great plan for the day?"

Pearl clapped her hands again. "Pearl likes that."

Bree slipped the well-used videotape out of its case and inserted it into the ancient VCR. The familiar sounds of the opening credits brought a smile to Pearl's face and she bounced up and down on her bed, completely ignoring Bree.

Bree checked in on John Huffman next. His time on earth was nearing an end. In her profession, Bree had learned to read the signs. John had been basically comatose for almost a month. Family members had been gathering around his bedside over the last few weeks, issuing their final goodbyes. It would all be over soon. She checked his vitals, fluffed his pillows, and readjusted his feeding tube before stepping back into the hall.

"Hey, got a minute?" Leslie asked as she approached Bree from the end of the hall. Her ponytail had slipped from its elastic and her eyes were wide.

"Uhh ... I just finished my first rounds. I should probably check on Florence again, but I can help if it's quick." *Truthfully, I just can't convince myself to stay away from Landon.* "What's going on?"

"The record player in the game room stopped working. Mr. Hansen is on the rampage because he can't listen to his record."

"How am I supposed to help with that? I hate to tell you this, but fixing technology—especially old technology—isn't one of my best skills."

"I thought maybe you could talk him down while I find another activity for the ones who just sit and listen."

"Have you tried playing the piano for them? Sometimes they like that?"

Leslie started shaking her head before Bree finished her sentence. "I tried that. Mr. Hansen wheeled over and slammed the cover of the piano down on my fingers. He broke two of my nails and I just barely got my manicure two days ago! I'm not that bad of a player am I?"

"You're a fine player. He doesn't know what he's doing. I'll go talk to him."

Inside the game room, chaos had erupted like Bree had never before seen at Shady Elms. She'd witnessed spats between patients, and residents acting up individually, but the situation in the room that day bordered on riot status. Mrs. Beth sat in her wheelchair in the corner, sobbing into her hands. A nurse knelt next to her, offering reassurance.

One patient continuously hit her cane on the table where three others were trying to play a card game. Mr. Carlisle, the man who could do no wrong, stood by the bookshelf, tearing pages out of the large print books while a frazzled male nurse tried to grab them from his hands. Another nurse ran around the room, doing her best to calm everyone down as she hurried from one patient to another. In reality, her wild flight just added to the chaos.

"I think you underestimated your assessment of the situation," Bree hissed at Leslie as she made a beeline for Mr. Hansen on the opposite side of the room. His voice stood out the loudest in the pandemonium.

"Mr. Hansen." Bree said his name loud enough to make herself heard over the commotion behind them. "Let's talk about what's wrong. There's no need to yell."

"There most certainly is a reason to yell," he bellowed as he crossed his wrinkly arms and puffed out his chest. Bree knew at his size and age, it was the most threatening pose he could muster. "*She*," he pointed at Leslie across the room, "broke the record player and now I can't listen to my music. I always listen to the same song in the morning. It's tradition. How am I supposed to listen to my favorite song?"

His voice grew in volume as he jabbered and pointed. Bree whispered her response, hoping her calmness would rub off on him. "I'm sorry the record player broke and I promise we'll get it fixed as soon as we possibly can."

"I want it fixed now!" he yelled.

Bree held her place and composure and continued to speak in a quiet voice. "Let's check the CD collection. Maybe we can find the same song on a CD."

"We've already checked. The only way to listen to my song is on a record player." Mr. Hansen pounded his fists on the piano.

Knowing he could hurt himself, Bree slowly reached out and grabbed his hands. "Let's go for a walk, just you and me. I want you to tell me all about your favorite song. There must be a great story behind it."

Rage still filled Mr. Hansen's eyes, but he stopped yelling and allowed Bree to gently push his wheelchair away from the piano and toward the common room exit. Just as they reached the doorway, Landon appeared from around the corner, pushing his grandmother in her own wheelchair.

Florence took one look at Bree and scooted to the edge of her seat, reaching her arms out as if beckoning to Bree. "Beware the Ides of March!"

# Chapter 10

**B**ree gasped, staring at Florence's outstretched arms. Her mouth moved as she tried to come up with a response, but she didn't know what to say. Next to her, Mr. Hansen launched into another one of his rants, pulling her attention back to the current situation.

Landon took in the scene unfolding behind Bree with a shocked expression. "Is it always this crazy around here?" he yelled over the commotion.

"I don't like the noise!" Florence cried, covering her ears.

"Trust me. This is a first. Shady Elms is usually quite calming for the residents. Just give us a few minutes and we'll have everything back to normal. I promise." Bree hoped the stress—and fear—consuming her didn't show in her voice.

"I hope so. We transferred Grandma here because we thought it would be a good atmosphere," Landon said with a hint of worry in his voice.

Bree frowned and glanced at Mr. Hansen. "We had a mishap with the record player and it won't play anymore. Mr. Hansen here is upset because he can't listen to his favorite song. It started a domino effect, if you will."

Landon looked at Mr. Hansen. "What's your favorite song, sir?"

Mr. Hansen told him the name of the song and then stuck his lips out in a pout. "I listen to it every day," he snapped.

Before anyone could say anything else, Florence began to shuffle her feet back and forth on the foot rests of her wheelchair, humming a tune to herself. At first, it was too quiet to interpret, but soon her voice grew louder and her humming was replaced by words. It was Mr. Hansen's favorite song.

Mr. Hansen stopped yelling and watched Florence for a few moments. Bree wondered if the old woman's singing would appease him, but before long he puffed out his chest again. "I want to hear it from the original singers!"

Florence closed her mouth and folded her arms over her chest, refusing to look anyone in the eye.

Bree glanced at Landon, embarrassed that all the problems of her life had been front and center for him to witness over the last couple of days. She prided herself in keeping her patients and job orderly and that day, March 15th, had turned out to be a complete failure. Landon didn't seem fazed by the unfolding events as he stared at his phone.

*Always business with that one. I'm not sure how I feel about that.* "I'm going to take Mr. Hansen back to his room. I'll be back to help in just a few minutes," she said as she started to walk away.

Landon reached out and grabbed her arm, his eyes still on his phone's screen. "Hold on a second." He finally looked up, only he turned to Mr. Hansen instead of Bree. "Is this what you want to hear?" He pushed a button on his phone and the familiar song—one she heard in the common room every day—began to play through the speaker on his phone. He turned the volume up as high as it could go.

Bree glanced at Mr. Hansen through the corners of her eyes. His shoulders relaxed and he closed his eyes as he slowly swayed back and forth to the music in his chair.

"Let's wheel you somewhere so you can listen to it," Bree said as she gently pushed him into a corner of the common room. "See? There's no reason to get worked up. Things always work out."

Mr. Hansen closed his eyes again, still swaying to the music. Bree smiled as she watched the peaceful expression on his face. She didn't know why the World War II era song meant so much to him, but she did know he'd served in the army. Maybe it brought back memories of his time in the service.

One thing Bree knew for sure about the residents of Shady Elms was that they all had a past. She'd heard their stories from family members or the residents themselves. They had families, they had jobs, they'd found love and lost love, they'd experienced tragedies and they'd experienced triumphs. The shell of a body each person lived in while at Shady Elms didn't do their past lives justice.

One day Bree would grow old just like her patients. Every day she hoped and prayed the nurses and family members who took care of her remembered her as vibrant and alive rather than whatever condition she would be in during her last days. And then treated her accordingly.

"This is kind of a catchy tune," Landon said as he pushed Florence farther into the room, still holding his phone up in the air.

"They all love listening to it," Bree answered. "I understand it was pretty popular back in the day. You'd be surprised at all the music I've learned since I started working here."

As the song continued from the first verse, to the second, to the third, the commotion in the room dimmed as the other nurses gained control over the residents. Bree felt herself relaxing, too. "*Thank you*," she mouthed to Landon who still stood in the middle of the room, phone held high, grinning from ear to ear."

"Grandma," Landon said as he stepped to the front of Florence's wheelchair. "May I have this dance?" Without waiting for a response, Landon took both of her aged hands in his and began bouncing back and forth to the music. Florence's face lit up and she attempted to match his moves from the comfort of her wheelchair. Soon, Landon let go of her hands and began pushing her wheelchair back and forth in rhythm with the song, even spinning her around a couple of times.

From the edges of the room, the other residents laughed and sang along with the words. A few of them joined in the dancing. Bree couldn't help but smile. Never had a mid-Sunday at Shady Elms been so entertaining.

Too soon, the song ended. Groans could be heard coming from the couches, chairs, and newly established dance floor. Mr. Hansen pushed himself up from his wheelchair and yelled, "Play it again!" The other residents joined him, yelling for an encore.

Fearing another riot, Bree caught Landon's eye. "Please?" she said, pleading with her eyes.

Landon looked down at his phone and then addressed the room. "I'd be happy to play the song again, but I have a request first."

Bree exchanged glances with some of the other nurses in the room, including Leslie. She had no idea what he was about to say, but she feared it might have something to do with her. Her fears were correct.

"If I play the song again," Landon began, "I want Nurse Bree to dance with me."

Bree's mouth dropped open. She didn't expect that. Dancing came easy for her, and she enjoyed it, but her job had never been a place where she allowed herself to let loose. At work, she tried to remain calm, sophisticated, and mature.

"Dance ... dance ... dance ..." the residents chanted in unison. Bree could distinctly hear Leslie's voice among the others and picked her as the recipient of a glare.

Leslie only shrugged her shoulders and chanted louder.

Before she could refuse, Landon left his grandmother's side and took Bree by the hand, leading her to the center of the room. He pushed the play button on his phone again and then set it on a table. He slipped one arm around Bree's waist and lifted her other hand up.

She put a hand on his shoulder and grinned. "Let's do this."

Landon didn't waste any time getting into the groove of the music or feeling Bree out as a partner. As soon as the voices began to sing, he took off across the room, bouncing and swaying, dodging wheelchairs and residents as they went. The others in the room clapped in rhythm as they danced. Bree had never felt so alive. She felt the bun loosen from the top of her head and her red hair cascaded down, flying in the air as she twisted and turned. It had been years since she'd danced like that, but her dance steps perfectly matched Landon's, as if they'd been partners for years. She threw her head back and laughed when he spun her around and around.

The song ended for the second time and they fell into each other, both laughing as they tried to catch their breaths. His arms came around her in a tight hug. She returned the hug, aware of every part of him that touched her. The feeling scared her.

Afraid that her feelings for him showed on the outside, she pushed against his chest and took a step back. "Th-thanks for helping to calm everyone down," she said breathlessly.

"No problem. I enjoyed myself. I had no idea long term care centers could be so entertaining."

"Trust me. You have no idea."

"Now that I'm aware of their charm, maybe I'll spend more time visiting my grandmother."

"Patients rarely get too many visitors."

Landon took a step toward Bree, his hand outstretched, but she stopped him. "I should probably go check on my patients again. It's been a while and there are some who can't be left on their own for long periods of time. If Florence is in here, I'll come back and check on her last ... if that's okay."

"That's fine." Landon looked over his shoulder. "Judging by her smile, I think we'll be in here for a while still."

Bree retreated from the common room, needing to get out before her trembling knees gave out on her. As soon as she rounded the corner, she grabbed for the wall and leaned against it, closing her eyes and forcing herself to take deep, calming breaths.

"Are you okay?" Leslie's voice brought Bree's eyes open again.

"I'm fine. Just letting the adrenaline wear off."

"What was that all about in there?" Leslie said as she leaned against the wall next to Bree.

"What do you mean?"

"In all the years I've known you, I've never seen you smile like that."

Bree stared at her feet. "I don't know what you're talking about."

"Ha," Leslie exclaimed. "You like him. A lot."

"He was just helping me out. You should be grateful to him, too. He's the one that calmed everyone down in there."

"I'm grateful, but I'm not swooning. I think you've got drool coming out of your mouth."

Bree instinctively put her hand to her mouth and then glared at Leslie. She reached up and began twisting her hair back into a bun on top of her head. "I'm just a project to him, remember?"

Leslie shook her head. "That's not what I just witnessed."

"I'm sorry you see things differently. I know you think I should change in order for guys to like me, but I can't do it. I've tried many times and it never works. I can't let myself fall for someone who doesn't like the real me ... luck and superstitions and all. It's not fair to me and it's not fair to them. Landon has made it very clear that he thinks my beliefs are ridiculous. I can't pursue him. End of story." Bree turned and hurried down the hall before Leslie could respond.

*Why am I so upset? I just had the time of my life in there and I'm mad. Why?* "You're mad at yourself for falling for someone you can't have," Bree whispered to herself.

# Chapter 11

**B**ree made a quick visit to John Huffman's room before peeking through the window of Pearl Lerner's room. The woman still stared, as if in a trance, at the show playing on the television. Judging by the scene on the TV, Bree had just enough time to check in on her other patients before Pearl would be ready for another adventure. She hurried back to the common room, knowing the rest of her patients had been present for the song incident.

It didn't take more than a single turn of the head to see that Landon and Florence were no longer there. Bree felt some relief from that knowledge. Her feelings toward him made her nervous.

"Mrs. Beth?" Bree said, interrupting the story she told a group of wary listeners. "It's just about time for lunch. Can I help you back to your room so you can be ready when it arrives?"

"Yes, dear. That would be fine," Mrs. Beth answered.

Bree pushed the wheelchair down the hall as Mrs.

Beth launched into a story about raising a pig for the county fair when she was eight years old. The pig started out as the runt of the litter, but after she bottle fed it, he grew into a healthy size with perfect proportions. The pig's name was Walter. After the fair—at which Walter won a blue ribbon—Mrs. Beth's father threatened to butcher him.

Mrs. Beth had told the story many times before and Bree knew the details by heart, although she'd always wondered how much of it was real and how much was a memory of a certain children's book getting mixed up with reality.

Bree pushed Mrs. Beth's wheelchair under her small table. "There you are," she said as she tucked a blanket around the woman's legs. "According to your clock," she pointed at the wall, "lunch will arrive in about five minutes. I'll check on you after you're through eating."

"Thank you, Bree. You remind me so much of a girl I once knew. She and I used to—"

"I'm glad I can be of help. I'll see you soon," Bree said, cutting the woman off as she slipped out the door. They parted that way every time Bree left the room. Sometimes she felt guilty for cutting the woman off, but if she didn't, she'd never be allowed to leave.

Back in the common room, she knelt next to Mr. Carlisle and waited for him to acknowledge her presence. He looked down and smiled at her with a vague look in his eyes. "Mr. Carlisle, I'm going to take Pearl outside to the picnic tables to eat lunch. Would you like to join us out there today?"

Mr. Carlisle smiled and nodded—all he ever did— so Bree helped him stand and tucked her arm in his as she escorted him through the building to the backyard picnic tables. The weatherman had announced it would be the warmest day of the year so far and Bree didn't doubt him. She loved spring days, even when she'd been warned by little old ladies to 'Beware the Ides of March.'

On her way back to Pearl's room, she passed the kitchen staff making their noon deliveries and instructed them to leave two meals on the back patio for Mr. Carlisle and Pearl.

At Pearl's door, she once again peeked in the window. The movie had ended and the credits rolled. Pearl danced about her room in her floral nightgown and yellow slipper socks as the final music played. Seeing her chance, Bree inserted her key and opened the door, quickly shutting it behind herself. Pearl tried to make a move, but Bree moved faster.

"Remember how I told you we'd go outside after lunch?" Bree said.

Pearl bobbed her head up and down.

"Well, what if we eat your lunch outside? Would that be fun?"

"Yippee!" Pearl squealed and bounced up and down on the balls of her feet. "Pearl loves eating outside."

"We'll need to trade your slippers for real shoes," Bree said as she opened a drawer and pulled out a pair of socks.

Pearl flopped onto her bed and pulled her slippers off, throwing each one across the room in excitement. One landed in the sink and one slid under the small dresser. Bree couldn't help but smile as she slipped socks onto Pearl's feet and then helped her into her brown leather slip-on shoes.

"Pearl's ready!" the woman yelled as she hopped off the bed.

"Let's put a jacket on you first," Bree instructed, helping the woman slip her arms into a thin windbreaker.

Pearl hurried to the door and stood as if standing on the starting blocks at the beginning of a race. Knowing the precision it took to make it out of the room successfully, Bree took her time. First, she pulled on the key ring attached to her wrist and inserted it into the lock, turning the key until she heard a click. Then, she pulled the key out and grabbed Pearl's hand in one swift movement. As soon as she turned the knob on the door, Pearl pulled her into the hallway and made a beeline for the back patio. Bree hung on for dear life, doing her best to slow the woman down so she wouldn't run over anyone during her hasty retreat. Once outside, Pearl could run to her heart's content. There were no gates in the yard area and the only way out would be back through the patio doors.

"Wahoo!" Pearl yelled as she hurried down the two patio steps and ran straight for the back fence.

Mr. Carlisle still sat at the picnic table where Bree had left him a few minutes before, only now two covered food trays sat on the table next to him.

Bree raised her eyebrows at him. "Why haven't you started eating yet? Are you feeling okay?"

"It's not proper to eat before all the guests have arrived," the old man whispered.

"I see." Bree sat down on the bench next to him. "If you wait for Pearl to tire and sit down, your food will be cold. In fact, it might even be dinner time. I don't think she'll mind if you start without her."

With a nod of his head, Mr. Carlisle took the cover off his plate of food and began to eat—mashed potatoes, cut up grilled chicken, and peas. Bree glanced at her watch. Only an hour until her break and she could eat the lunch she'd packed. Every time she ate lunch at the nursing home, she relished in the fact that she could still chew all her food.

The warm sun on her face felt so good, she tilted her chin toward it and closed her eyes. Pearl still ran around the yard and Mr. Carlisle made quiet chewing noises next to her. Until the weekend, she'd loved her life. When Landon showed up, she realized how nice it would be to have someone to share it with. Unfortunately, he wasn't going to be an option after that day.

"Hey, Bree," a male voice said.

Bree opened her eyes as one of the other nurses seated his patient next to Mr. Carlisle. "Hi," she answered. "It's Harvey, right?" They didn't usually work the same shifts, but every few months, they worked a Sunday together.

Harvey nodded. "Yep. Good job calming everyone down in the common room this morning."

"It wasn't me. The grandson of one of my patients is the one who saved the day." Next to her, Mr. Carlisle dropped his fork on the table. Bree picked it up and gently placed it back in his hand.

"Either way, I'm glad it didn't get too out of hand," Harvey said.

"Speaking of that patient, I need to check on her. Will you be out here for awhile? Pearl isn't done running yet." Bree pointed at her patient across the yard.

"We'll be here," Harvey answered. "I planned on reading to Mr. Shupe. Mr. Carlisle, you're welcome to listen in. Pearl is one of my patients when you're not on shift so she and I get along great. I don't mind keeping an eye on her."

"Thanks, I'll try to hurry." She turned to Mr. Carlisle who was stabbing at the peas on his plate with his spoon. "Mr. Carlisle, I'll be back to help you inside soon, okay?"

He smiled and nodded before returning his attention to his peas.

Inside, Bree slipped into the restroom before heading to Florence's room. She fixed the bun on top of her head for the third time that day and put on some lip gloss. *What's wrong with you? Stop liking him!* She glared at herself in the mirror before opening the door and continuing her walk down the hall.

"How's everything going in here?" she asked as she entered Florence's room.

"Grandma just finished eating and is requesting a nap," Landon said. "I thought I might grab a bite to eat while she sleeps."

Bree crossed the room and helped Landon as he assisted Florence into her bed. The woman didn't look at her much until her head hit the pillow. When their eyes connected, she bolted up. "Beware the Ides of March! Beware the Ides of March! Beware the Ides of March!" she chanted over and over.

Bree took a step back. "Florence, I'm not sure what you mean by that. What do you want me to do?" She forced her voice to sound normal, rather than come out in a squeak—which is what it wanted to do.

Florence finally lay back against her pillows again and reached for Landon's hand. "I want my picture."

Landon's forehead crinkled. "Your picture?"

Florence pointed at the dresser on the opposite side of the room. "In there."

He took three steps and opened the top drawer. Bree kept her distance, not wanting to upset the woman yet again. She watched as he shuffled through the contents of the drawer before pulling out a small photo album. "Is this what you want, Grandma?"

"Please bring it over here," Florence said in a raspy voice.

No one in the room spoke as the elderly woman gingerly turned each page of the album. From Bree's position in the room, she couldn't see any of the photos, but she didn't dare leave, either. She wanted an explanation for the warnings against her.

Near the end of the album, Florence stopped turning pages and pointed at a picture in the book. "It's you," she said, turning to Bree. "Beware the Ides of March."

Bree took cautious steps as she approached the bed and leaned over the side. Florence's finger still pointed at the picture, but her eyes bore into Bree as if she could see her soul. When Bree saw the photograph, she gasped. She'd seen the exact same photo before—many times.

"You," Florence said as she pointed at the red-haired girl in the photograph. "Me," she said, pointing to a girl standing next to the redhead.

"It all makes sense," Bree whispered, mostly to

herself.

"Maybe you could explain it to those of us—namely me—that don't understand what's going on," Landon said.

"Florence," Bree began, "that's not me in the photograph. That's my grandmother. Janey Donovan. I've seen her copy of the photograph before. This is when she played the part of Calpurnia in the city theater's rendition of Julius Caesar, right? Did you play the part of Portia?"

Florence grinned. "I'm Portia."

Bree threw her head back and laughed. "No wonder you kept warning me." She looked up to see Landon grinning at her—his dimples more prominent than ever. "I told you so," he whispered. "Nothing to worry about."

Bree rolled her eyes and then pulled a chair closer to Florence's bed so she could sit down. "Can you tell me more about the play? My grandmother had the time of her life. She told me about it many times. Were you good friends with her?"

Florence closed the photo album and stared at the ceiling as if searching her memory. "Janey Donovan ... No one quite like her."

Bree relaxed against the back of her chair and listened as Florence retold the antics of the two young women. They'd met shortly after Mama Donovan moved from Ireland and became fast friends. When Florence's husband joined the military, they moved out of the city and eventually lost track of each other.

Florence reached for Bree's hand. "I hope you have the luck of the Irish because Janey sure did."

# Chapter 12

**W**hen Bree left Florence's room a short time later, Landon followed her out the door.

"Hey, do you ever get any breaks?" he asked.

Bree glanced at her watch. "It's time for my lunch break right now. I just need to return a couple patients to their rooms first."

"Can I take you somewhere for lunch?"

Bree wanted to tell him that she'd packed her own lunch and would just eat in the break room, but her brain didn't convince her mouth before it spoke. "Sure," she answered.

They drove to a fast food place a block from Shady Elms and ordered their food before choosing a corner booth. "Do you go home from work exhausted every night?" Landon asked.

Bree pulled a napkin from the container on the table and wiped her fingers. "Yes ... but it's a good kind of exhaustion."

"You love your job."

"I really do." She nodded.

"You're good at it."

Bree tilted her head back and forth. "Most of the time. You witnessed one of the rare times things didn't go as planned in the common room this morning. Of course, we can blame that one on Leslie. Her patient is the one that started it all."

Landon shrugged. "It all worked out in the end."

"Thanks to you."

"Happy to be of help."

They chewed and chatted and laughed, sharing stories from their youth and adult years. Not once did the subject of luck or superstition come up in conversation. For once, Bree felt like they were actually getting to know each other and not just looking at specific personality traits. She liked it.

Back at the nursing home, Landon reached out and took her hand, sending shockwaves trailing up her spine. She stared at their hands and then at him.

"I've been working on something for you. I'll give it to you before you leave tonight. You get off at five, right?" Landon asked.

Bree swallowed hard. "What is it?"

"It's a surprise, but I think it will be helpful to you."

❧❧

The afternoon dragged. All Bree could think about was Landon and the surprise he had for her. Guys didn't usually give her things. At least, not guys she only knew for a few days. All five of her patients opted for long afternoon naps and when they were awake, chose to read or watch TV. Time seemed to slow down.

"Everything okay?" Leslie asked when they passed in the hall on the way to fill out their final reports for the day.

"I think so," Bree answered.

"What kind of an answer is that?"

"An honest one."

"That guy is messing with your mind. I've never seen you like this. At first I thought it was a good thing, but now I'm not so sure."

Bree raised her eyebrows. "Do you see my dilemma? He seems like a good guy. He's fun to be with, but ..."

"But?"

"I can't be with someone who doesn't like me the way I am."

Leslie shifted her clipboard from one arm to the other. "I feel like we've had this conversation before."

"Trust me, we have. Many times."

Leslie gave Bree a hug. "I'm here to support you, however this all works out."

"I know," Bree said, returning the hug. "I may end up as an old maid and become a patient here myself. Will you still support me then?"

"Of course. I'll help you get dressed and I'll buy you ugly nightgowns and I'll make sure the kitchen only serves you soft foods."

"Gee, thanks."

Footsteps approached from behind the two nurses. "Every time I see you two, you're hugging. I'm starting to get jealous."

Bree let go of Leslie and stepped back at the sound of Jason's voice.

"Hi, honey." Leslie stood on tiptoes as she planted a kiss on Jason's lips. "I just finished up so we can go."

Landon came out of Florence's room and walked toward them. "You're not even going to say hi before leaving?" he asked Jason with a wide grin. "I saw you walk by through Grandma's window."

"I didn't know you were here," Jason said as he shook Landon's hand. Unlike Leslie and Bree, the guys didn't hug. Landon kept one hand tucked behind his back.

"We're heading back to Leslie's for dinner. I'm cooking. You two are welcome to come," Jason said.

Landon glanced at Bree. "I'm game. You?"

"Uhh ... sure."

"First," Landon began, "I have that thing I promised you."

Bree felt her face turning red and hoped it wouldn't be anything embarrassing since Leslie and Jason stood nearby.

"Here," Landon said, pulling his arm out from behind his back.

Bree looked at his hand. He held a red-covered report folder. "What is it?"

"My final assessment. You promised me two days to prove to you that I'm right and you're wrong. I'd never finish a job without writing up a final report."

Bree stared at him with her mouth hanging open. Her greatest fears had just come to fruition. Landon had no interest in the 'real' Bree. No one said anything as Bree reached out and slowly took the red folder from his outstretched hand. The only thing less appealing than having her personality faults laid out in report form was having them laid out while she had an audience.

Taking a deep breath, Bree opened the cover and read the first headline, carefully written in black ink: *Reasons Why Bree Is Wrong and I am Right.* Skipping the paragraphs below it, she turned the page and read the next header: *Ways to Help Bree Become a Better Person.* Hot tears formed in the corners of her eyes and blurred her vision. She couldn't read any more— nor did she want to.

She couldn't look Landon in the eyes so she stared at his chest. "I'm glad you find me so entertaining. You can keep this." She shoved the folder back into his hands and turned to Leslie, who stood with a confused look on her face. "I'm sorry, but I'll have to take a rain check on dinner. See ya Tuesday."

Without giving anyone a chance to respond, she grabbed her purse and bolted from the building. She heard Landon call her name, but she didn't turn around.

# Chapter 13

**B**ree managed to keep the tears from falling while driving home on Ogden's streets, but alone in her apartment, the emotions of the weekend flooded out. Curled up on the couch, with a soft blanket and a chocolate bar, she berated herself for falling for Landon even when she knew it would end in disappointment. She tried not to be mad at him. After all, he'd clearly stated on their first date that he would be using her as a project. Instead, she spent the entire weekend trying to pretend that wasn't his real intent. And in the process, she let her heart open to someone who didn't feel the same way as she did.

Her phone buzzed over and over inside her purse, but she ignored it. She couldn't talk in her condition and didn't want to anyway. "Stupid boys," she whispered. "I don't need a guy. I'm doing just fine on my own."

Willing herself to stop crying, she stood from the couch and splashed cold water on her face in the bathroom. She refused to look at her pitiful self in the mirror. "Dinner. I need dinner," she told herself.

Inside the kitchen, she made herself a cold turkey sandwich with lettuce and tomato and cheese. Her stomach growled as she peeled a banana to go with it. She'd almost made it to one of her barstools next to the kitchen counter when she stepped on something sharp. A trickle of blood immediately dripped from her heel. She grabbed a tissue and wiped away the blood, revealing a tiny shard of glass. "Landon's stupid broken mirror," she said aloud. "Thanks for adding a gazillion years of bad luck to the years I already had."

She turned on her TV and immediately went to the DVR. The documentary about St. Patrick's Day was still there, but she didn't have the heart to watch it.

Delete.

Nothing else on the DVR looked interesting and the TV proved the same.

A knock on the door pulled her attention from the TV. She had no intention of answering the door in her condition. She hit mute and waited, hoping the 'intruder' would go away.

Another knock.

She took a bite of her sandwich and stared at the door.

"Bree? Come on! Open the door," a voice called.

Landon.

"No way," she whispered. "That ship has sailed."

"You didn't even read the report before you stormed off," Landon called through the door.

Bree rolled her eyes and took another bite.

"If you open the door, I can explain everything."

Bree stayed put at the table. Across the room, her phone buzzed in her purse again. She walked across the room, tiptoeing to avoid stepping on her tender heel, and pulled her phone out. Just as she expected, Landon was calling from the porch. There were six missed texts and eight missed calls. Two of those calls were from Leslie. Even Jason had tried once.

"Sorry guys. Tonight, it's just me." She turned the phone off and dropped it onto her couch, flipped off the lights in the kitchen, and retreated to her bedroom. One look at the alarm clock on her bedside table told her it was only seven o'clock.

She kicked off her shoes and climbed into bed in her work scrubs. *No such thing as too much sleep.*

On Monday, Bree woke at six a.m., much earlier than usual, but not surprising considering how early she crashed the night before. She performed her morning ritual, stretching each part of her body carefully before rolling over and swinging her legs over the proper side of her bed.

But then she stopped.

Landon had been wrong to try to change her, but many of the things he'd said were true. *Am I really going to have a bad day if I get up on the wrong side of the bed? Probably not.* She continued to sit on the edge of her bed, contemplating different aspects of her life. Many of the things that made up her daily rituals were a force of habit rather than fear or superstition. *Maybe if I try loosening up—and changing it up—I won't have to rely so much on luck. If I change, I want it to be because I made the choice myself, not because someone told me to.*

With new determination, she lifted her legs and swung them over the other side of her bed, standing up before she changed her mind. "Ha!" she said aloud. "Take that, givers of luck."

She spent the rest of the morning trying to determine which of her habits were fears, which were superstitions, and which were just plain habits. She found herself smiling as she showered, ate, and cleaned up her apartment. When she turned on her phone, she smiled and shook her head when she saw the additional missed calls from Landon and deleted the messages without listening to them.

"Bree Donovan can be herself without anyone telling her what's normal," she proclaimed to the empty room.

After lunch, she grabbed her purse and keys, determined to accomplish her errands without thinking about a certain guy. She slipped her lucky rabbit's foot inside her pocket just before opening the front door. *Nothing wrong with wanting a little luck.*

As she opened the door, something fell to the ground at her feet. She jumped back in surprise. When she realized what it was, she gritted her teeth. The way she saw it, she had two options. She could either read the report in the red cover Landon had so kindly left at her door, or she could walk it to the recycling bin and forget he—or the report—ever existed.

She chose option number two.

Her day continued in that manner. She felt alive and invigorated and found herself amused when things didn't go her way. When a car driving by splashed dirty water on her ankles she laughed. "Just the luck of the Irish," she told the man on the sidewalk next to her who looked on with concern. When she opened the carton of eggs she bought at the grocery store and found two of them cracked—they'd been fine in the store—she made an omelet instead of frowning. When she finished a load of laundry and found her white scrub top had turned pink thanks to a stray red sock, she laid it out on her kitchen counter and drew hearts on it with puffy paint.

"Make your own good luck," she whispered to herself. Mama Donovan used to tell her that all the time. Bree always interpreted it as doing everything in her power to avoid items or events that would bring her bad luck. But maybe that wasn't what Mama Donovan had meant.

That night, she fell asleep with a smile.

⋙⋘

"Just because you were mad at Landon didn't mean you couldn't return *my* phone calls," Leslie said as she dropped into a chair next to Bree at the nurse's station on Tuesday morning.

"I'm sorry," Bree said and then smiled for added emphasis. "I needed a little time to myself. I'm fine now."

"You are? So you talked to him then?"

Bree shook her head. "Talked to who? As far as I'm concerned, last weekend never happened. It's St. Patrick's Day today—my favorite day of the year. For the sake of the Irish, try to have fun today. I plan to."

Leslie opened her mouth to say something, but

112

Bree cut her off.

"I'm off to see Pearl. Oh, and make sure you check your clipboard carefully. I put in a request to trade patients. I'll be Mr. Hansen's nurse now since you and he don't exactly get along." She tucked a pen into the pocket of her shamrock covered scrub top and started down the hall.

"Wait … who do I get?" Leslie called to Bree's retreating figure.

"Florence," Bree called over her shoulder.

Bree visited her patients with a bounce in her step that morning, happily taping leprechaun cutouts on the walls of each of their rooms. She played a card game with Mr. Carlisle and even got him to say a few words. She combed John Huffman's fine white hair, making every strand have a place, even though he never woke to say anything. She listened to an entire story told by Mrs. Beth about the time she visited Scotland for St. Patrick's Day and didn't even correct her about it being the wrong country. She danced an Irish jig with Pearl while listening to Irish folk songs. And most importantly, she got a smile out of Mr. Hansen.

After making two full rounds of her patients, she slipped out of Pearl's room and turned around. Her breath caught in her throat when she saw who stood there.

"Did you read my report?" Landon asked quietly.

Bree swallowed hard, trying to keep the knot in her stomach from growing bigger. "No. And I don't plan to either."

"Can I read it to you?"

Bree raised her eyebrows. "I'm not six. Besides, I

113

threw it away. I don't need someone telling me what's wrong with me." She turned and started to walk away, but Landon put a hand on her shoulder, stopping her.

"Exactly. If you would have read the report, you would have seen that I agree with you," he said. "Don't worry. I made a copy before I left the original at your house on Sunday night."

Without allowing Bree the chance to say anything else, he opened another report folder, green that time, and began to read. "First heading: Reasons why Bree is wrong and I am right. Bree thinks luck is what makes her successful. However, she went to college and got a degree in a career she loves. After observing her in her work environment, I see that she excels at her chosen career. She works with kindness and patience and betters the lives of those she helps each day. Conclusion: Bree doesn't need luck to be successful—she already is." He cleared his throat before continuing.

"Heading number two: Ways to help Bree become a better person. This consultant's recommendations for a better Bree are threefold. First, she should immediately stop her search for a guy and date Landon," he stopped reading and glanced at Bree. She stood, frozen, with her arms crossed over her chest. "Second, she should promise to let him spoil her and make her laugh. Third, she should keep her personality as is because it's perfect the way it is."

Bree felt as if her insides were on fire. Never in her life had a guy said things like that to her before. She sensed they weren't alone and turned to see Leslie and two of the other nurses listening to Landon's declarations.

"Bree," Landon continued before she found the words she wanted to say. "I've dated a lot of girls. Some for a long time and some for not so long. It never worked out with any of them. When I first met you, I wanted to convince you to be like all the other girls I'd ever dated and that was completely wrong of me. After all, I'm not with any of those girls for a reason. Our personalities didn't mesh. According to you, last weekend should have been the unluckiest of my life because of all the rules I broke. But it wasn't. It was my luckiest because I met you. I want to be with you just the way you are. Will you give me chance?"

Bree wiped a single tear from her cheek. "Of course, but only if you promise not to make me break any more mirrors. I stepped on leftover glass last night," she said with a shake of her head.

Landon grinned, showing off his dimples. "I have something else for you." Without any other warning, Landon dropped to one knee in front of Bree and pulled out a ring box.

Bree's stomach flip-flopped as she stared at his hand. The alarm bells in her mind went off again. *Is he insane?* Behind her, the small crowd that had gathered to watch Landon beg for forgiveness gave a collective gasp and began to whisper.

"Will you accept this? I spent Sunday night and Monday morning before work, and then half of last night looking for just the right one."

"I ... I don't ..." Bree stuttered. "We just met and ..."

Landon stuck his arm out farther. "Just take the box, Bree."

With trembling fingers, she reached out and took it from his hand. She held her breath as she unclasped the lid and opened it. Inside, on a velvet cushion, lay a perfectly formed four-leaf clover. "You found one!" she cried.

"You said you've been looking your whole life. A little bit of luck never hurt anyone, right?" he said as he stood and slipped his hands around her waist.

She closed the lid of the box and wrapped her arms around his neck. "When you were in Ireland, did you kiss the Blarney Stone?" she whispered.

Landon leaned back to get a better look at her. "We never had time for that. Why?"

"Because, I'm going to kiss you now, and I wouldn't want to catch a lip fungus. Just think of all the people who have kissed it. Eww."

Landon threw his head back and laughed before picking her up and swinging her around as he kissed her.

When he set her down, she could barely stand on her own. "I think my luck has changed," she whispered.

# ABOUT THE AUTHOR

Tifani Clark grew up on a farm in southeastern Idaho (yes, that's where they grow all the potatoes) as the middle of five children. She had a lot of space to imagine and daydream and often pictured herself as a character in one of the many books she read. She was habitually found pretending to be Scarlett O'Hara. She is married to the love of her life and is the mother to four fabulous children. When not writing, she enjoys playing the violin and piano and traveling to new places. She especially enjoys visits to national parks and places of historical significance.

www.ingramcontent.com/pod-product-compliance
Lightning Source LLC
Chambersburg PA
CBHW060635130626
46555CB00002B/818